APPLE BLOSSOM TIME

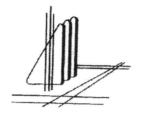

APPLE BLOSSOM TIME

Behind the Clouds the Sun is Shining

Don C. Davis, ThB, BA, MDiv

Archway Publishing books may be ordered through booksellers or by contacting:

Archway Publishing
1663 Liberty Drive
Bloomington, IN 47403
www.archwaypublishing.com
1-(888)-242-5904

Because of the dynamic nature of the Internet, any web addresses or links contained in this book may have changed since publication and may no longer be valid. The views expressed in this work are solely those of the author and do not necessarily reflect the views of the publisher, and the publisher hereby disclaims any responsibility for them.

Certain stock imagery © Thinkstock.
Any people depicted in stock imagery provided by Thinkstock are models, and such images are being used for illustrative purposes only.

The New English Bible – Oxford University Press

Revised Standard Version of the Bible, copyright ©1952 [2nd edition, 1971] by the Division of Christian Education of the National Council of the Churches of Christ in the United States of America. Used by permission. All rights reserved.

Scripture taken from The Living Bible copyright © 1971 by Tyndale House Foundation. Used by permission of Tyndale House Publishers Inc., Carol Stream, Illinois 60188. All rights reserved. The Living Bible, TLB, and the The Living Bible logo are registered trademarks of Tyndale House Publishers.

Scripture taken from the King James Version of the Bible.

Cover inspiration by Nolan Davis

ISBN: 978-1-4808-1340-3 (e)
ISBN: 978-1-4808-1341-0 (sc)
ISBN: 978-1-4808-1339-7 (hc)

Library of Congress Control Number: 2014920854

Print information available on the last page.

Archway Publishing rev. date: 3/10/2015

ACKNOWLEDGMENTS

A Place In the Story is the best of positive future-vision fiction, inspired by successful achievers.

Inspiration for my novel in seven sequels, *A Place In The Story,* has come from multiple sources, but none greater than from my wife, Mary, and our sons, Charles and Nolan, and their families. Mary, whose own success story continues to inspire her family, has been my devoted supporter and skillful editor. Along with these, there is the continuing influence of having parents who were good people.

The overview nature of my books has come from a list of writers whose books and articles explored the future, advanced knowledge, shared their knowledge base from science and technology, inspired positive insights, and led the way to a knowledge-based faith.

Those who have had a major influence on my thoughts and paradigms include: Norman Vincent Peale, Napoleon Hill, Albert Schweitzer, Og Mandino, Carl Sagan, Norman Cousins, Bill Gates, Fulton Oursler, Dale Carnegie, Theodore Gray, Norman Doidge, Martin E. P. Seligman, Michio Kaku, and others, whose vision is a reference to the future more than to the past.

From these, I have gathered an overarching view of the future. Like an impressionist painting, these provide a bigger picture of our place in the story for sunrise tomorrows.

To: Dr. James Kelly *james/maria@crx.com*

From: Steve Kelly *stevekelly@crx.com*

Dear Granddad,

One of your grandchildren who sat on the farmhouse porch and listened to your stories a few years ago, has stretched his education across extended years in these changing times. Yes, I am a part of that new dynamics in which college graduates are having difficulty finding the right career opportunities. Therefore, I am belatedly entering a Masters Degree program.

Many universities are involved in having their students combine academics and service. It's the same here. So, I am a volunteer with "Teens Second Reach." I have become acutely aware that many young people get caught in situations that trap them in bad decisions made out of conflicting identities.

So, Granddad, have you ever given thought to writing a story that will help troubled teens find their way back from deep disappointment - a story that could help them think their way through to positive solutions for negative situations? It's not that there are not books already out that can help, but I believe your positive philosophy of making healthy choices could be immensely helpful.

If I had a book of stories with your positive philosophy, I could share it with students to help them put a new beginning beyond old endings.

Do you have some suggestions for me?

Your Grandson,

Steve

To: Steve Kelly *stevekelly@crx.com*

From: James Kelly *james/maria@crx.com*

Dear Steve,

Do I have some suggestions? Yes. The story you want is in my novel already in progress. It's the Ru Dallin and June Hyland story. It shows how my book, New Tomorrows, helped Ru turn old endings into wonderful new beginnings.

In this book I tell how the turning point influence my "New Tomorrows" book of stories has a positive influence on the life of the troubled young Ru Dallin. I won't say more about the book except that it leads to a wonderful and beautiful ending. I don't want to spoil it for you when you read it. I'll send you a copy as soon as it is published.

Your asking about my writing such a story has given me extra motivation to move ahead quickly. So, I'll be at the farmhouse for the next few days finalizing a little novel called, Apple Blossom Time.

And, congratulations on being involved in your service program. Remember that business phrase, 'doing good while doing well?' It can also read, 'doing good while doing academics.'

Granddad

CHAPTER ONE

Uphill Journey

THE UNPAVED ROAD, THAT LED THROUGH THE MOUNTAIN VALLEY, followed close by a rippling creek of clear water. Weeds and grass were growing between the routes made by cars and pickup trucks traveling along the mountain road. The little road forked just before one well-worn set of tracks led across a bridge up to and past the apple shed, where for many years the sign above the apple shed porch had read in big bold letters, DALLIN'S APPLE SHED. Out beyond the apple shed, the little road led to the two-story house where Ru's grandparents had once lived. Oak trees surrounded the house so much that only the front of the old classic house was clearly visible. An artist painting a picture of that mountain setting, in Norman Rockwell style, would have shown Dallin's Apple Shed in the center of the painting, with baskets of red and yellow apples sitting on the edge of the porch, and Ru's grandparents sitting there in rustic chairs, ready to help customers who came in their pickup trucks to buy the best apples and cider in Jonas Ridge.

In the close-up foreground, the artist would have shown the old wooden bridge that crossed the creek, with handrails on each side made from slender oak saplings. That old wooden bridge was where Ru Dallin and June Hyland had sat on the edge as childhood playmates, letting their bare feet dangle in the water rushing underneath.

That picture had changed now. Ru's grandparents had died and left the apple shed and tree-surrounded house as cherished memories from yesterday. On this day, Ru was all alone, but in a hurry when he stopped on the bridge and leaned against its wooden rails just long enough to listen and watch the water trickling down the creek. The sound of the rushing water grew dim as Ru turned back, and without crossing the bridge, began walking up the fork in the road that followed the creek up the valley to the home of June Hyland, and her parents, John and Marie. Ru zipped his light tan jacket up that was jostling in the springtime wind. In a vivid color contrast to his tan jacket, his blue plaid shirt framed the strong and slender body of a restless high school boy.

As Ru approached the John and Marie Hyland house, their youngest daughter, June, was sitting on the porch of the big two-story white weatherboard house, waiting for him. She was ready to help him with his math homework, where doing math took second place to their just being together as special friends.

After the homework was finished, Ru lingered on the porch, swinging around the porch post hesitantly a couple of times, before stepping down off the porch, and linking their goodbyes to the next time they would meet, saying, "See you at the school bus stop in the morning."

Instead of going back home by way of the road that followed the creek, Ru decided to take the shortcut up across the hill and through the apple orchards. He climbed the hill slowly as he made his way among one of the best kept orchards in the whole valley. The Hyland orchard was well-pruned and ready for the spring spraying.

When Ru came to the top of the hill, he stepped over the long row of stones that formed a kind of fence and sat down on the stone wall. On down the hill from there the apple orchard was different and in considerable contrast to Mr. Hyland's orchard. It was a major contrast to what it would have been if it had still shown the handiwork of his late granddad. This section of the adjoining orchards now belonged to Ru's Pa. The trees had not even been pruned since those days when his granddad had given to the orchard careful attention. As Ru sat on the stone wall and looked down the hill through the neglected trees, his mind raced back to the delightful days when he and June had played here among the apple trees as childhood playmates. At five years old, they had romped through the orchards many times while Ru's granddad was carefully pruning the apple trees. June had made up a silly little game that she and Ru played together in apple blossom time, trying to catch apple blossoms on their tongues as they floated in the wind. Whether or not they ever caught any didn't matter so much as the fact that, in their own way, were playfully dancing in the wind. Their special friendship continued year after year as they met each morning at the school bus stop, just down the road from where Ru lived with his Pa.

Things were so different now. The apple shed sat empty. The stately old two story house where his Pa had grown up in his youthful days, sat empty. The bungalow house where Ru lived with his Pa showed signs of long neglect. Adding to that sense of bygone yesterdays, Ru's mother had left and said she was never coming back again. Ever! Ru felt the loss deeply.

As Ru sat on the rock fence between the two orchards, he stared down the hill at the house where he and his Pa lived, remembering the fierce argument his mother had with Knute before she left. His Pa accused Roxanne of hanging out and drinking beer with that man from Texas more than she stayed at home. "So what," she said angrily. "It's better than being here with a man who is drunk every week-end and barely makes a living at that old sawmill. We never have any money beyond just getting by. Don't even have a television or phone. If you had any ambition, you'd take care of the apple orchard and this farm your dad left for you. Instead of that, you're just letting it run down and grow up in weeds. Some future I would ever have here. I'm leaving the day we sign the divorce papers, and never coming back!"

"But what about Ru?" Knute had argued back. "Don't you care anything about him? He needs you here."

"Yes, I care. That's about all I care about here. I hate to leave him, but I just can't stay here. He'll inherit the place here some-day, if there's anything left worth having after the way you have abandoned it. It's all in your dad's will. And after I sign the divorce papers it will go to him someday. So, yes, I will sign the paper and then I'll be gone. I want no part of it. You've broken every promise you ever made to me and have treated me like dirt. I'm sick of it all. I'm leaving here. Ru will be better off that way. But if you don't change your ways, he may end up just like you."

Ru remembered that after that bitter exchange of words, his Pa didn't say a word, just looked hurt, picked up his bottle and ambled out on the old porch of their bungalow and sat down.

The memories of that day crushed the joy out of Ru's mind as he sat on the old stone wall looking down the hill through the run-down orchard. But it only took a moment for his mind to shift back when he thought of how he and June had chased the apple blossoms in the wind and had sat on the edge of the bridge, dangling their feet in the running water.

Ru got up and ambled down the hill through the trees. *"I gotta do something,"* he was saying to himself. He remembered the days when he turned twelve and his granddad had let him help prune the apple trees. Mostly he just picked up the limbs that his granddad cut off. But there were times when his granddad taught Ru the art of cutting away the inner limbs so the fewer limbs left could get plenty of sunshine and produce those beautiful red and yellow apples. What Ru had liked most about working with his granddad in the warm September breeze, was picking the apples and then packing them in baskets and putting a row of them on the edge of the porch of the apple shed. Ru remembered the sweet fragrance of the apple cider they made when he helped turn the crank of the cider mill. The aroma of the apple shed and the fragrant smell of the cider was still vivid in his mind. People used to claim that Arthur Dallin's apples and cider were the best one could buy anywhere in Jonas Ridge. Maybe it was true, but Ru wondered if some of how delicious they thought his granddad's apples were had something to do with the picture people saw as they crossed the bridge and drove up to the apple shed to buy apples, and then sat on the porch and talked with his granddad.

When Ru got to the bottom of the hill near the apple shed he was tempted to go sit on the edge of that old porch. But the memories were too intense. He wished his Pa would make a change and make the old orchard blossom again. The people who had really cared about him were gone now. His granddad had died suddenly three years earlier, and his grandmother two years before that. And his mother had left and not been heard from since. All of that was in the past and only a set of memories. He remembered his granddad looking up across the hillside and admiring the orchard. As Ru walked down the hill and reached the little dirt road, he turned an looked up across the hillside that now showed years of neglect. He wished his Pa would make it blossom again.

Ru's feeling of loss and disappointment were made even worse one day when he walked down the road from his house to the local gas station and country store. He was standing around outside beside the vending machine and about to put his money in, when he overheard some of the men inside, who were sitting around the old pot bellied stove, talking about his Pa. "Knute Dallin is just letting his dad's place go to nothing. He's run through the money his dad left him and he's never done one thing to keep up the orchard. He could have had one of the best orchards here in Jonas Ridge if only he had taken care of what his dad left to him. The bottle is ruining him. And I don't know what will happen to his son, now that Knute's wife has left and gone off with that man who came in here from Texas."

It was all Ru could take. He had come down for a Pepsi. Now he didn't want one. He just turned and walked back up the road beside the creek, back up to where his Pa was sitting on the porch, reading a book.

"What cha reading?" Ru asked, as he walked up and sat down on the wooden steps of the old green shingled bungalow house.

"Can you believe it, Ru?" he said. "That new preacher over at Pine Grove Church came to see me a couple days ago. I told him he was wasting his time if he thought he was going to get me in his church." I said, 'You don't even want me in your church!'"

'Getting you in the church is not the name of the game that I play,' the preacher said. 'It's helping people. It's caring about what a person's story is shaping up to be, and the possibility that I can help in some small way to make it better.'

"I liked what he had to say. He talked about life, not religion. And before he left he went out to his car and got this book for me." I said, 'I can't pay you for it.'

'Don't want any pay.' he said. 'If you'll read it, it's yours for free.' "There was no prayer. No little sermon." The preacher said, 'The book is not all that religious. It's stories about choices and self-improvement. Like the Book of Proverbs, it's about risks and rewards – about finding a way to live so life has more payoff and fewer penalties. So, Knute,' the preacher said, 'I really like to look at life in terms of just being a friend to everybody whoever they are.' As he got up to leave he said, 'That's sacred.'

So I thanked him as he left, then came back up here and started reading his book. Makes a lot sense. It's different."

"What's it called?" Ru asked.

"It's NEW TOMORROWS. New Beginnings Beyond Old Endings. Interesting. Makes you feel different about life. You'd like it too. When I finish you can read it."

"Okay," Ru said, and got up and went inside.

CHAPTER TWO

Changing Winds

RU WAS ABOUT TO TURN SIXTEEN, AND VOWING TO QUIT SCHOOL JUST as soon as he reached sixteen. June tried to talk him out of it. "Nobody can do without a high school diploma," she argued.

"I can," Ru argued back. "If my Pa won't do anything with this place, I will."

Ru looked off into the distance as he talked to June more seriously than she had ever heard him talk. "I have begged Pa to quit drinking and make something of the farm like the other apple growers in the valley, but it's of no use. Depending on Pa to make a change seems hopeless. Maybe it's time for me to see what I can do."

A few days later, after Ruben had milked the cow and turned her out into the pasture, his Pa came walking up in front of the old faded red barn. "Ru," he said, "Look up at that hillside. Tell you what we are going to do. We are going to make that orchard blossom again the way it used to every springtime.

Hardly sure of what he was hearing, Ru said, "You mean it, Pa? You mean you are going to start work on the orchard?"

"That's right. And not just the orchard. Ru, you see that line of trees on the hillside just beyond the orchard. Some day you are going to see that hill up there covered with green grass and black angus cattle grazing on it. That's where we are going to cut the trees and turn it into pasture land and start raising black angus cattle."

"But, Pa, you said, 'we.' You mean we can work together?"

"Exactly! From now on you have a different Pa and the two of us are going to be partners."

Ru's imagination was fired up. Partners. He could already see it in his mind. He could see the whole hillside hanging with red and yellow apples, and cattle grazing on the pasture beyond. He could see the apple shed come alive again with baskets of apples sitting on the edge of the porch and people driving up to DALLIN'S APPLE SHED to buy them.

It was no surprise the next morning when Ru's Pa drove the old green Chevrolet truck up to the front of the house and stopped. He slid out the door and leaned across the truck bed and called, "Ru, get the chainsaw off the porch there and put it in the back of the truck. By apple blossom time we are going to have that hill cleared off. We'll sell the logs to the sawmill and then buy some more black angus cows to go with the two we have."

Ru turned quickly and picked up the chain saw with one hand, swung it around, and bounded down the old plank steps, as though the weight of the saw was no more than an empty milk bucket. "Coming, Pa," he said as he hurried down to the truck. He swung the chain saw into the truck bed beside an axe and climbed in beside his Pa. "Pa, you really mean it, don't you? We are going to clear that hill off and put cattle there?"

"You mighty right, son. We done let things go on too long without making this place produce. We'll have to start small at first, maybe four or five black angus cows, but it's time you and I really started making this ninety acre farm worth something. You see where the apple trees stop off? Up there is some cleared space just before you get to the tree line. I figure we can set out about five rows of new trees there and start us a young orchard."

"Sounds great to me!" Ru said. "I'm with you all the way."

"I like to hear you talk like that, Ru. I thought I could count on you and those strong muscles, cause it's going to take a lot of work."

Ru didn't care how much work it would take. He was excited about the future. He felt like his Pa had just announced him as a partner - as a man.

They cut trees all morning, sawed off the logs into the right lengths, and trimmed the laps enough so they could make a long row of the brush. Mostly Ru manned the chain saw and his Pa cut and pilled the laps. When lunch time came, they went to their house and fixed up what Knute called grub, and then headed back out to the hills as soon as they had eaten and stacked away the dishes that they would take care of after supper. They didn't think bachelors had to be so fancy and wash dishes after every meal, so they washed them only after supper. Things didn't stay as nice as they had been before Ru's mother had left Knute and gone off to Texas with that other man she claimed was just a friend. It had been a bitter ending of a relationship, and even though his Pa would have denied it, Ru could tell that he missed her, in spite of their conflicts and battles.

When they got back out to where they were clearing the trees, Ru took over the chainsaw again. A couple hours later, his Pa insisted that he run the saw and give Ru a break. So Ru took the axe, went up the hill and began working with the brush.

Knute had just called "timber" to let Ru know that another tree was about to fall, when Ru heard a big, aowwwee! Ru rushed down to the trunk of the tree. Even before he got there he could see that the tree had kicked to one side, The tree had his Pa pinned against another tree. The chain saw was still running. Ru reached over and turned the chain saw off and said, "Pa, how bad are you hurt?"

There was no answer. "Pa. Pa!" Ru called.

"Pa!" Ru called louder and frantically, but his Pa didn't even move. Quickly Ru got a pole and lifted the tree off his Pa's chest.

"Pa, can you hear me? Answer!" Ru was becoming frantic in the face of the possibilities.

"Pa. Oh, no. Pa." Ru burst into tears and dropped down on his Pa's limp body and cried. Then he put his ear down to his chest to see if he could hear his heart beating. He wasn't sure. Talking aloud, he said, "Pa. I got to get you to a hospital!"

They didn't have a phone at the house, but even if he could call, it would take too long for an ambulance to arrive. Ru ran to the pickup truck and drove it up to the edge of the woods and opened the door quickly. He rushed to his Pa and gathered his limp body up into his arms and carried him to the truck. When he got him inside, he propped his head up with an old jacket and closed the door. When he got in on the driver's side, he dropped his head down on the steering wheel and cried in gasping sobs. Then he started the truck and headed down by the orchard, past the house, and out onto the dirt road and onto the winding paved road. Once out on a bigger highway he moved at high speeds until he got to the county hospital. He followed the sign to the Emergency Room entrance and began blowing his horn as soon as he got to the entrance. Immediately two men came out with a gurney and began to take Knute inside. Ru walked along beside them.

"What happened?" one of them wanted to know.

"He got crushed by a falling tree," Ru said.

Once inside, the men began rolling the gurney through double doors to another room. "You can wait here," one of them said.

Ru sat down in a waiting area, leaned forward and put his hands up against his cheeks. He got up and walked over to the door of the emergency room, but it was closed. The sign said, "Staff Only." Ru came back and sat down.

When the door from the emergency room finally opened, a doctor and nurse came out together. The doctor sat down beside of Ru and put his arm around his shoulder. "It's too late, son," he said. "I hate to tell you, but he's already gone."

"I thought so," Ru said, through his broken sobs. "He never moved after the tree hit him. He never knew what happened."

"I'm so very sorry it happened." the doctor said.

"He was going to clear the whole hillside off by apple blossom time," Ru said, as he buried his face in his hands.

CHAPTER THREE

Saying Goodbye

RU COULD SEE THE CARS PARKED AROUND THE LITTLE WHITE PINE Grove Church as he came riding over the top of the ridge in the family car provided by the funeral home. It was little consolation to him that his Uncle Hale and Aunt Mertie were riding in the back seat. In fact, he resented their presence. Since they had arrived they had acted like they were now his overseers. He didn't know why they should feel so much like his guardians now. They had never paid any attention to him before. He also hadn't liked it when they pressured him into buying a nicer casket for his Pa. He knew he couldn't afford it and knew his Pa wouldn't have wanted it. But there was little he could say when his Uncle Hale said to the funeral director, "Figure it in. I'll pay for it." Ru didn't like it - made him feel so useless and unimportant to have his uncle come rushing in to take over like that. There seemed to be little use to try to buck the offer.

"Oh, it's such a darling little church," Aunt Mertie said when she looked down the valley and saw it. That didn't describe it for Ru. To him, even though he hadn't gone there much, and his father almost never, only twice that he could remember, to Ru that little church was a symbol of what was right in the world. It couldn't be described by the word, darling. Dignity, strength, and faith were words it suggested to Ru, especially now. He knew that white frame church was an important part of the John Hyland family, and that made it important to Ru. They were there every Sunday. There was no more respected man in Jonas Ridge and the whole valley, than John Hyland. Ru appreciated that now more than ever, especially for the way he had stood by him and been so supportive in the past two days since Pa had died.

Ru choked back the tears when he saw the tent on the hillside beside the white church and knew it was there he would have to say a final, good-bye, to his Pa. He hoped the preacher would make it all short and easy and not make him cry before all those people. It was hard enough for him to hold back the tears now as he rode down the mountain road, across a little bridge and up in front of the church.

There was not a large crowd at the church and it took only a minute for Ru and his Uncle Hale and Aunt Mertie, and a few distant relatives, to file in and take their places in the pine pews, down front, across the aisle from the pall bearers.

Reverend Morris motioned for the people to be seated, once the family had come in and taken their seats. The service opened with the choir singing a song Ru remembered hearing one Sunday when he had gone to church with John Hyland's family. He remembered that his granddad was there that Sunday, as usual. It was

a song Ru had never gotten out of his mind. He was glad to hear
it again and followed every word.

> In the bulb there is a flower;
> in the seed an apple tree;
> in cocoons, a hidden promise:
> butterflies will soon be free!
> In the cold and snow of winter
> there's a spring that waits to be,
> unrevealed until its season,
> Something God alone can see.

Ru listened when Reverend Morris read from the scriptures.
But his attention was even more focused when he began to tell
about an incident that Ru had never heard about. "Knute Dallin
was a man trying to find a higher fulfillment of manhood and
being a father, when he was killed so suddenly. He was in the
beginning of a new phase in his life. I know about that new phase
because I was there when it began.

I went over to see Knute a few weeks ago and found him sitting on the edge of the porch of his house. It was cold enough that
the sunshine was welcome. I sat down beside him and we talked.
Knute let me know very quickly that he wasn't about to come to
church just because I had come to see him. That's when I assured
him that wasn't my mission at all – that what I wanted to do was
to be a friend to everyone in Jonas Ridge. We talked for a while
about this and that. After a while we got around to talking about
how, all any of us have is, a place in the story, and how everyone
is writing a part of that story. That's when I mentioned a book of

stories that I thought he might like to read. He didn't object. So I went out to the car, got the book, and gave it to him. The title is *NEW TOMORROWS*, with a sub-title of *New Beginnings Beyond Old Endings.*

Explaining briefly, I said, 'This new beginnings thesis is in each of the ten stories in the book, built on the Big Ten words that define our best qualities, and that they can be chosen by anyone, anywhere, anytime as identity markers that lead to our best life.' I said, 'They are not religious words, just turning point words for turning failure upside down and beginning anew.'

A few days later I saw him again out at the shed near the orchard where he was making some new fence posts. I stopped by and we stood in the sunshine on the south side of the shed and talked. I remember that conversation like it was only yesterday. He said, 'I been reading that book you gave me - made a lot of sense, and made me start thinking about my story - how it hasn't been all that good. I got the sense that I could still write a good story. But, I still am not ready to be religious. In fact, I been thinking about one sentence in the book where it says, 'God is not a religious word.' It's like one doesn't have to be religious to be good. The book talks about the Big Ten qualities we can choose to define who we are trying to be. I've tried to memorize them, you know -kindness and caring, honesty and respect, etc. I'm sure you know them. So what I have decided is that I am going to create my own story using those words.'

Knute paused a moment then put the fence post aside and said, 'Ru says he is going to quit school the day he turns sixteen, and that's just a few days away. I don't have room to say much. I quit, too, when I was his age, much to the disappointment of my Pa.

I know that if Ru quits school, he'll get restless. I need to find
something for him to do.'

I said, 'Knute, you think a lot of that boy, don't you?'

'Sure do,' he said quickly. 'I haven't done much to show it, but
that's going to change - going to be different from here on. I'm
turning over a new leaf. I'll have to admit the book you gave me
helped - helped me a lot. I got to prove to him, all too late I know,
but I got to prove to him that, like the book says, people can turn
old endings into new beginnings. I don't want to say anything
about it until I can show that I am serious. You'll see. And I hope
Ru will see.'

It was obvious Reverend Morris was near the end of his me-
morial tribute when he spoke slowly and deliberately. "Knute
Dallin was deep into that new beginning the day he was suddenly
killed by that falling tree. That's the Knute Dallin I want us all to
remember."

Ru listened as Reverend Morris brought his short talk to a
close. But the part about his Pa's new beginning was what Ru kept
recycling in his mind. Ru knew in his own way, that even in such
a short time, his Pa was making a new beginning. He had changed.
As far as he knew, he hadn't taken a drink for several days before
that day they went out to cut trees and clear the land. Ru knew
clearing that new land was a part of his new Pa.

When the service was over it was a mixture of heartbreak
and celebration as Ru followed the casket down the aisle and
then up to the cemetery. There Reverend Morris read from a
little book and then said a closing prayer. Reverend Morris came
over and shook hands with Ru, and with the few people seated
under the tent, then came back to Ru. When he reached out his

hand again, Ru stood up and they walked away and down the hill together.

Marie Hyland must have left immediately after the service in the church ended, for she was already at the house when Ru and a few others gathered there in the Hyland family home. She had some cake, coffee and tea ready, along with other foods the neighbors had brought in. Still eating a piece of pie, Uncle Hale and Aunt Mertie stepped out onto the porch where Ru was sitting on the edge of the long porch of the Hyland, turn of the century style house.

"Ruben," Hale said, as he reached down and laid a hand on Ru's shoulder, "Mertie and I have talked it over and have decided that you can come and live with us."

Ru was surprised at that kind of response from them. They had no obligations to do so. Mertie was his mother's sister, but his mother had walked out on him and his Pa and Ru assumed they had just been cut out of the family.

"No, I'll just stay right here," Ru said, trying not to sound too blunt, as he declined.

"But you can't do that, Ruben," Mertie put in. "You can't take care of yourself out here in this wilderness."

That brought a quick rush of defensive emotions, the way she called this place a 'wilderness'. He knew they had looked down on his Pa and his little old house for a long time. That attitude was coming through now in what she said. In his mind this was no wilderness, especially in the last few days since his father had painted a picture in his mind of how the place would soon be a thriving orchard and cattle farm. Now it was a place of security and the promise of the future.

"Look, Ruben," Uncle Hale said, "We will give you a nice room and you can get a job, maybe help me at the car lot, and make good for yourself. You will have far more opportunities than you can ever have out here. And I know of several other places I can get a job for you."

"But what about the farm? What about the cows?" Ru questioned.

"How many cows do you have?" Uncle Hale asked, degradingly.

"Well, we have just three cows now, but Pa." Ru stopped without finishing the sentence, uncertain as to whether he should reveal the plans he and his Pa were working on.

"So?" Uncle Hale retorted.

"Well." Ru paused. "Well, Pa and me, we were gonna clear up some more land and get several more cows."

"How many cows do you think a fellow would have to have to make a living up here? Thirty? Forty? And how long would it take to get a herd?"

"I don't know," Ru said. "But there's the apple orchard. We were gonna take real good care of the trees this Spring, spray them and be able to sell apples and cider by Fall."

Uncle Hale responded without really hearing. He said, "Yes, but, how is a fifteen year old boy going to live between now and then? You need to come and live with us. You need someone to cook for you and some way to make a living. You'll starve yourself to death out here."

"You gotta come," Aunt Mertie put in. "We can't have you staying up here all alone. What will people think?"

In his own mind Ru was saying, '*I don't care what people think!*'

Ru got up and ambled down the steps. "I don't know. I'll think about it," he said, as he went around the corner of the house and started up the hill behind the house.

"Remember, Ruben," Uncle Hale called after him, "you'll have a hard time making it out here by yourself."

Ru kept going up the hill, then sat down on the stone wall between the orchards of John Hyland's place, and what was now his place. He wanted to be alone so he could think. He didn't trust his uncle and aunt. He never had. His Pa had always resented them - said they were too damn good for the rest of us.

The three cows were grazing far down the hill in that narrow strip of pasture between the creek and the apple orchard. Those two beef cows and one milk cow looked different to Ru now. Ru's excitement about the future he and his Pa had dreamed, came back into his mind just by looking at the two black angus cows down there. They already had a start on Pa's dream. Suddenly the rush of emotions hit him. His Pa was gone now and he was left alone with the dream. Tears blurred his vision as he looked up beyond the valley at the cascading hills that surrounded Jonas Ridge. He guessed he could have twenty acres of orchard up here and maybe twenty acres of pasture beyond the orchard. But then the crushing emptiness of being left alone hit him again. He swallowed hard and turned and looked in the other direction.

Far up the valley he could see John Hyland loading hay onto a trailer. Ru wanted to talk to Mr. Hyland. He walked down through the orchard, turned up the little road and went out to where Mr. Hyland was. He trusted him to give some good advice.

"My uncle and aunt want me to go live in the city with them," Ru said, with no more introduction than saying hello to Mr.

Hyland. "They say they will give me a room in their house and that I can get a job. But I don't want to go. I don't want to leave this place - don't want to leave the dream Pa and I were building together - more pasture land, and taking care of the orchard the way Granddad did. But that dream seems to be gone now."

"Yes, and I am sorry about that," Mr. Hyland said. "But maybe the dream can go on in some way. I wonder, Ru, was it all your Pa's dream? Wasn't it partly your dream, too? And, from what the preacher said, your Pa was working on it for you. Is that what you understood?"

"Yes, the dream was our dream." Ru responded thoughtfully. "Now part of it's gone forever. And Uncle Hale wanted to know how many cows would it take to make a living out here? We have two beef cows now, but no money to buy more now."

"Tell you what, Ru. You just let the cows run with mine for a while until you can see your way forward. You can go to the city and see how things work out, and if you want to come back, we'll just turn the cows back over into your pasture. How's that?" Mr. Hyland offered.

"That's surely nice of you, Mr. Hyland," Rufus answered. "That will give me time to think things through a bit more. But I really don't want to go. I can see, though, that they aren't going to let me stay out here by myself, so I guess I'll have to go." Ru thanked Mr. Hyland for his advice as he started back down the road beside the rippling creek.

The full impact of what he had decided didn't hit him until he went to his room and began to pack some things. He began to feel the immense sadness of his Pa's death, combined with leaving the only place he had ever known. It seemed too much like being caught up in the wind of a storm and being swept away. His actions were saying, go. But his heart was saying, stay.

Ru wished he had a better suitcase to put his few clothes in, but the old beat-up brown case was all there was. His mother had taken the better one. So he had to use an old cardboard box for some of his things. Though he was embarrassed about it, it was in keeping with the old quilt on the iron bed and the unpainted walls of his room. His dresser was an old wash stand that had been handed down through his Pa's family.

Having to hunt for some covers for the hide-a-bed, that was folded out from the couch for his uncle and aunt to sleep on, was equally embarrassing. He guessed they would be equally uncomfortable with having to stay overnight. He knew they were used to much finer things, and they even talked about going to a nearby motel, but decided they would need to stay with Ruben for the night.

It was a cold night and Ru got up twice during the night to put some more wood in the old stove, being as quiet as he could, since his uncle and aunt were sleeping in the same room. He knew they slept in a place much warmer than this one. Ru filled the stove again at daybreak and opened the draft. His uncle and aunt were already up. Ru got the milk bucket and headed for the barn. It was bitter cold and the wind whipped the snow flurries around. With the ground getting white in grassy spots, it was the kind of day that his Pa hadn't gone to the sawmill, but laid around the house, hitting the bottle off and on all day long. Only recently he had stopped drinking and had begun to do some work around the farm. It was obvious now that his Pa had begun thinking in a new way before that day he was crushed by a falling tree.

Just as Ru reached the barn, the thought hit him, '*If I milk the cow, what will I do with the milk?*' He decided to go ahead and drive the cows over into John Hyland's pasture and milk the cow over there.

Steam huffed from the cow's nose as they walked through the blowing snow. At the edge of John's pasture, he let the bars of the gate down and drove the angus cows through. Then holding the rope, he led the milk cow to Mr. Hyland's barn.

"Yes, we can use the milk," John said. "Marie makes butter to sell to regular customers, who are always wanting more than she has to sell. Some people still want country milk and butter enough to be willing to drive all the way out here to get them."

Before Ru left, John shook hands with him and wished him well in the city. "Remember, Ru," John said with kindness, and very intentionally, "If I can be of any help to you, all you have to do is call on me. I think a young man in your particular shoes right now could find himself needing a helping hand once in a while, and I will be glad to be that helping hand."

"That means a lot to me, Mr. Hyland," Ru said. "I just might need it sometime. Thank you!"

As Ru got near the Hyland house, he saw June come rushing out, carrying her books, and starting down the drive on her way to the school bus stop.

"See you later, Mr. Hyland," Ru said quickly. "I want to catch up with June and tell her good-bye."

As Ru fell in step with June, he said, "I'm leaving this morning."

"Yes. I know. Dad told me that your uncle and aunt want you to go live with them. I hope you will like it in the city. You must be looking forward to living there," June said without looking up.

"No. Not really," Ru responded quickly. "What I'd rather do is stay right here, but folks say I shouldn't - that I should accept my uncle and aunt's invitation. I know one thing, June. I'm going to miss seeing you. We have been playmates and then class mates for all these years. Remember how we used to play in the orchard? Remember how you used to come to Grandpa's apple shed and help pack apples? And like this, we used to walk down to catch the bus together. It's going to be quite a change and I will miss it and miss you lots."

"And I will miss you a great deal, too" June said. "You will be going to school there, won't you? You shouldn't just quit school."

"That's what Uncle Hale says. I guess I won't have a choice. Here comes the school bus. I guess this is good-bye for a while. I don't know when I'll get back out this way."

June reached over and gave Ru a hug as she said good-bye, then stepped up into the bus. Just before the door went closed, she leaned back out and said, "Drop me a line, Ru. Let me know where you are."

Ru stood and watched until the bus went out of sight.

After the bus was gone, Ru walked up the road and stopped at the creek bridge near the apple shed and looked over into the cold water, rippling around the snow covered rocks with its trickle and swishing sounds. He knew he was saying good-bye to his boyhood, as he remembered fishing for trout in the creek many times. But it was too cold to linger long with his thoughts here. He zipped his jacked up more and turned his collar up as he started down the road and then up the drive to his house. He remembered that he had left his milk bucket at Mr. Hyland's house, then realized it didn't matter. He wouldn't be needing it anymore, anyway.

It wasn't very warm in the house and Ru started to put some more wood in the stove when Uncle Hale came in and suggested he not add any wood. "We'll be leaving as soon as we have some breakfast." Ru laid the wood back down on the floor behind the stove and closed the stove door with a bang. He didn't like the way his uncle kept giving all the directions. Once again he felt swept away by the winds of change in which he was no longer in charge of anything.

After breakfast, Ru gathered up his things in his room and put them in the box, ready to put outside on the edge of the porch. By now every sound was an echo. It seemed so strange to hear the sound of the door to his room clatter as he closed it behind him. Even his footsteps seemed to be strange as he walked into the kitchen.

"Ruben," his Aunt Mertie said, "I couldn't get the back door to lock."

"Oh, it's broken. We never lock it."

"But you must find some way to fasten it. Maybe you could nail it closed."

"I ain't nailing it closed," Ru responded quickly, feeling like everything she said was as harsh as the cold air blowing in the wind.

"You'll have to secure it some way," she said.

"Okay," Ru rebutted. I'll nail a button slat over the corner." The sound of the hammer seemed to echo in the cold mountain air as he closed the door and began to nail the slat.

Uncle Hale came in the front door rubbing his cold hands together, saying, "I just turned the power off at the main switch, and turned the water off under the house. I guess we are ready to go. Ruben, don't you think you need to drive the truck into the driveway of the barn instead of leaving it out? You got plenty of anti-freeze in it?"

Ru took the suggestion, going out quickly without saying a word. He ground the starter a bit on the old Chevrolet before it fired up. Once again that feeling of closing the door on an era of his life haunted him. He felt awkward just driving the truck into the barn. The old barn doors were hard to pull together, but he managed to get them closed.

By the time Ru got to the house, Aunt Mertie was locking the front door. "You sure you got everything, Ruben?" she quizzed. "Did you unplug the refrigerator?"

Uncle Hale interrupted. "It doesn't make any difference. The power has been turned off. Come on. Ru, put your things in the trunk of the car."

Ru accepted the key his Aunt Mertie handed to him, wishing he could have been the last one out of the house and to have been able to lock the front door. He felt like he was being pushed out of his own house. Tears came to his eyes and his voice broke. "I don't want to go. I don't see why I can't just stay here."

"Well, you can come out and check on things once in a while," Uncle Hale said.

Ru's emotions were pulling him back in one last effort to keep from leaving. It was of no use.

"Come on, Ruben," Aunt Mertie said. "You're much too young to live out here all by yourself."

She meant it in kindness, but it was a rebuff. 'Couldn't she have said it some other way,' Ru thought. His Pa had begun treating him like a man just before he died - took him in as a partner in new plans for the farm - a new beginning. Now he was being treated like a kid.

His resentment was in his body language as he grabbed his box of things and put it under his arm, and then took hold of the handle of the suitcase and swung it in the trunk of his uncle's new Buick. Before he got into the back seat, he paused a moment and looked across the orchard and to the hill where he and his Pa had been clearing land. He didn't say a word to his uncle and aunt, but to himself he was saying, '*Some day I'll be back and make the dream come true.*'

CHAPTER FOUR

Winter Winds

BARDEN HILL DRIVE HAD THE MARKS OF ONE OF THE FINER SECTIONS of the city. Nice houses stretched along each side of the street. Ru couldn't see why it was called Barden Hill since there was no hill around.

"Well, here we are," Hale said, as the car door handle clicked. You've never been here before, have you Ruben?"

Ru wanted to sound appreciative for what they were doing for him. "No, Uncle Hale. This my first time."

Ru felt as much out of place when he walked into their living room, as he supposed Uncle Hale and Aunt Mertie had felt in his Pa's mountain bungalow house. Ru was still just looking the room over and observing the carpet, furniture, and the white brick fireplace, that obviously had never had a fire in it, when Aunt Mertie said, "Come on upstairs, Ruben. I'll show you your room. You can have Leslie's room. She is in college and seldom comes home. When she does come home she can use the guest room."

Ru followed his aunt up the stairs, carrying his scarred up old suitcase and box of clothes. He had his old work shoes in the cardboard box, but realized that they would never fit in these surroundings. Ruben liked the blue carpet but despised the delicate bedspread with a matching pattern in the sheer pink curtains over the windows. He was glad when he noticed that draw draperies could be pulled over them. "I'll empty a couple of drawers here in the chest," Aunt Mertie said, "and let you put your things in. Then we can store your suitcase in the attic."

Ru knew his aunt was trying to be helpful and kind, but he felt very uncomfortable. He didn't know whether to sit down or stand up. Finally, he got his suitcase and swung it up onto the bed, but quickly realized that might not please his aunt, so he set it down on the floor again and opened it there and began getting out his blue jeans and plaid cotton shirts. He was wearing the only pair of dress pants he owned. When he began pulling off his coat, so he could move more freely as he worked, Aunt Mertie said, "Over here is a place for you to hang your clothes. Here, let me have your coat and I'll hang it up for you." Ru handed her the coat, wishing he could hang it up for himself. At least that would give him something to do to keep from feeling so useless and awkward. Ru was emptying his suitcase by putting things on the bed, when his aunt came over and began to take them and put them in the drawers, telling him which drawer to use for his socks and underwear.

Ru guessed his aunt had a reason for helping him put things away but he would have rather have been doing it for himself. As soon as what few things he had been put away, Aunt Mertie said, "Now, Ruben, the next thing we will need to do is go to town and buy you some casual dress clothes. You'll need new shirts and slacks, shoes and socks. And if you see a new sport coat that you like, we'll get that, too."

Ru was just about to offer not to get new clothes because of how much they would cost, when Aunt Mertie took that defense away saying, "Now, Ruben, don't you worry for one moment how much they will cost. If you are going to stay with us, we want you to dress nice and have whatever clothes you need."

There was no need for Ru to say anything about his own clothes being good enough to suit him; they weren't going to be good enough to suit his aunt, and he may as well get used to the idea. After all, he didn't want to cross her if she was anything like her sister. She and his mother seemed to be quite alike - taking over and making a person feel little - telling them what to do instead of asking. He guessed that was what his Pa resented most when his mother was still at home - her telling him what to do, talking and talking, until it was likely that Pa was fuming inside and just went outside to get away. She always wanted things nicer than Pa ever thought they had any need for. When she walked off, that was one of the things she went on and on about. "I can see that I am never going to have the things I want as long as I stay around here. So, I'm leaving and never coming back." She meant it about leaving. At times Ru could sense that Pa was glad for her to leave. Then right in the middle of one day she had packed up what she wanted and left. It was clear to Ru that she meant that part about never coming back, too.

It had hurt when she refused to come back to his Pa's funeral. It looked to him like she could have done that much, just for him, if for no other reason. Ru wondered why Aunt Mertie was doing all this for him - was she trying to cover-up for her sister's actions?

He wasn't sure. He just knew his Aunt Mertie was so much like his mother that there was no doubt they were sisters.

Ru was tired of shopping in the stores long before he had enough new clothes to satisfy his Aunt Mertie. He couldn't see any need for having six pairs of dress pants, and he certainly didn't need the white shirts she was buying for him. She did consent for him to get one yellow dress shirt to wear with the new brown plaid sport coat she was getting. Ru was puzzled. How could they spend that much money on clothes? They had gone to the best stores and each time his aunt would just say, "Charge it on my account."

That night after supper, as they sat in the den, he learned the 'why' for all the new clothes. His uncle brought his cup of coffee with him to the den, sat down and put his feet on the hassock. After his aunt had loaded the dishwasher and started it, she came in and sat down in a rocking chair. From the statement his uncle made, it was clear what the new clothes were for. "Ruben," he said, in a demanding tone of voice, "I went by to see the school principal and he agreed to let you start to school at the same level you were in Jonas Ridge. You realize how important this is, don't you?"

"Yes, sir," Ru replied in a compliance manner. He had made up his own mind to quit school. Now, however, it was obvious his decisions were not worth a 'hill of beans' here. His aunt and uncle were going to so much effort for him that he knew he couldn't say, no. After all, just the day before, as he and June were walking together to the school bus stop, she had asked him to start back to school. So now Ru made no protest – just simply asked Aunt Mertie what he should wear on the first day back to school.

Inside, Ru felt defeated. He just knew that any idea he might have about things was worth nothing unless it was also his uncle and aunt's idea, too. He tried to mute his feelings of disgust by picking up part of the newspaper and reading, like Uncle Hale had already begun to do.

That night, before Ru finally went to sleep, he lay on the soft mattress, dreading the next day. He dreaded to have to face the fact that he had planned to quit school and was going to school now because he was being pushed into it. Beyond that, he hoped the city boys wouldn't make fun of his country ways. But he was not about to be spared that. That first day, a loud talking boy called him an uncouth hillbilly. Ru said nothing in response, but he felt like knocking his teeth out, which he was sure he could do.

Two weeks later, he proceeded to try just that when a boy stuck his feet out and tripped him while he was walking down the aisle in the classroom. It was a foolish attempt, for in the next few minutes he and the other boy were walking into the principal's office where they were given a good talking and suspended for three days. Ruben knew that if his uncle learned about it, he would get another talking to from his uncle when he got home and have to face the music there. He hoped his uncle wouldn't hear about it and that he could leave the house the next morning like he was going to school, but then hang around downtown all day. That idea didn't work for one minute when his uncle came home from work. "Ruben," he demanded, "What's this I hear about your being suspended from school today?"

"Suspended?" Aunt Mertie put in, aghast.

"Yes, suspended," Hale assured her. "He and Jerome Crawford had it out in a fight right in the classroom."

"Not Jerome!" Aunt Mertie exclaimed. "I wonder how Henry Crawford will take that."

Ru didn't know Henry Crawford from anyone else, but he guessed he was Jerome's father and somebody important enough not to be crossed, judging from the worried look on his aunt's face. He didn't care who he was, one thing he had to make clear in that new school was that just because he was new and from the country, nobody was going to bully him around. He had to let them know he could carry his own weight or else he would never be accepted. He was just ready to explain that Jerome had tripped him, when Uncle Hale put in again. "Now Ruben, this kind of thing can't happen again, or you'll be out of school for good. You came pretty near blowing your opportunity today, so be sure it doesn't happen again. And, what's more, you make sure you don't get into any trouble with a black student. That would be the end of it. You understand that, don't you? Your aunt and I are giving you a real break and we expect you to take full advantage of it."

There was little Ru could say but, "Yes, sir."

From the way his Uncle Hale picked up the paper and began to read, Ru knew that he considered the subject closed, even though he had never been given an opportunity at all to tell what happened. He knew it was a serious offense in the eyes of the school officials, but he thought a man ought to have the right to take up for himself and be given a chance to state his reasons for what he did.

When Ru went back to school, he could tell a difference in the way some of the boys treated him. It seemed like he had earned a measure of acceptance among them. Sam Pless and Ray Scott asked Ru if he wanted to go with them to the basketball game on Friday night. It was the first time to be included in any outside activity and Ru accepted immediately.

They came by for him that evening and blew the horn on Sam's new Chevrolet. Ray got out and motioned for Ru to get in the middle in the front seat. As soon as they got about a block down the street, Ray reached over to the back seat and got a beer from a twelve-pack and stuck it in Ru's hand. "Here. Let's get in the mood before we get there." He got another one, opened it and handed it to Sam, then got one for himself. Ru went along and turned up his beer. When they got to the school parking lot, Sam drove out to the back side and backed into a parking space.

"Finished yours yet, Sam?" Ray asked, as he threw his own can out the window.

"Just about," Sam answered, then turned up the can, took another quick drink, and pitched the can out the window.

"How about you, Ru?" Ray asked, and without waiting for an answer said, "What's the matter Ru, can't you put one little old beer away faster than that?"

Ru thought their cans didn't sound empty when they landed on the pavement, but he couldn't be sure. Ru emptied his can and then accepted a second one and took a big swallow. It wasn't long before he was cracking silly remarks and talking loudly. He was ready for a third when Ray passed it to him. By the time they got out to go to the gym Ru was pretty well loaded. He didn't care any more. He was speaking to everybody on the walkway in front of the gym. When he got to the door he started to walk right through without paying.

"Hey you," the man said. "You gotta pay to get in here," Sam said. "Ru, give the man four dollars."

Ru fumbled in his billfold and got out four dollars and slapped it on the table. "Is that enough?" he said obviously too drunk to know for sure.

The game had already started as they climbed up the bleachers at the end of the row. Ru managed to get up pretty well but when halftime came and they went to get some refreshments he stumbled along. He had just pushed his way up to the drink machine when the police came up and told him to come with them, that they were taking him for public drunkenness. Ru looked around for Sam and Ray but they were gone.

By the time he got to the station he had his senses enough to realize that the police would be calling his uncle and aunt. He was angry with himself for being such a fool, drinking to much. He knew he had been set up. Besides being so foolish, he was scared. He had never been in any kind of trouble with the law.

He knew what would be coming from his Uncle Hale when he came down to bail him out the next morning. He dreaded it. His uncle and aunt were always so right and he was always so wrong. No amount of reason or excuse would be good enough. And yet, they were giving him so much. He couldn't put it all together yet.

Ru felt so guilty and ashamed when the jailer came and opened the door and told him his uncle had come for him. He didn't know what to say first. He figured Uncle Hale would be ready to wash his hands of him and send him back home. Maybe he could save him the trouble - just tell him straight off, that he was going to do that. He spoke first, lest he not get a chance later. "I'm sorry, Uncle Hale. I've caused you enough trouble. I'll leave and go back home." He didn't know what his uncle would have said if he hadn't said what he did, but saying it apparently hadn't taken the fury out of the storm.

"Come on," Uncle Hale demanded. "Let's go get in the car, if you are sober enough."

Once they got in the car, his uncle put his arm up on the seat, as though he were going to sit there and lecture him. But he just looked over sternly and then took his arm down quickly, reached for the switch key, started the car, and drove away without saying a word. All the way to the house, not a word was said. The silence was unpleasant. Though nothing was said, Ru figured it wasn't over yet. He was sure he would get chewed out just as soon as they got to the house. He was right about that.

"Sit down over there," Hale said to Ru as soon as they walked into the living room. "I've got to say some things to you, straight."

Aunt Mertie came into the room and dropped down into a chair without saying anything, while Hale walked over and stood in front of the fireplace. "Ruben, why do you treat us like this after what we are doing for you? I just don't understand how anyone in your situation can be so unappreciative. Why do you do what you do? Do you have to be like your daddy? Can't you realize what drinking leads to? One would think you would have sense enough not to do it yourself. What do you have to say for yourself?"

Ru just sat there with his head down. He wanted to say that he didn't want to be here in the first place, but knew that would only add fuel to the fire. He didn't have to look up to see the accusing looks he was getting. He could feel them.

"Listen, Ruben," Aunt Mertie said. "We aren't against you. We want to help you. We have spared no cost in trying to do that. But look what we are getting in return. Hale has an important business and what do you think this does for him to have his nephew get into a fist fight, then get arrested for drunkenness at a ball game? It's just more than we can take. If you can't do better than this, you'll have to go back home and do the best you can."

Ru cut in quickly and sharply. "All right! You don't need to say anything else. I'll go. I didn't want to come here in the first place. It was all your idea. Don't blame me."

"Who else is there to blame?," Hale cut in quickly and sharply. He walked across the room and took a seat. "We've given you a new opportunity, but we can't make you take advantage of it. You'll have to do that for yourself. I just got one more thing to say. "I'll give you one more chance. You've got to prove that you appreciate our effort or else we can't go on with it."

Hale got up and left the room and Aunt Mertie followed almost immediately. Ru guessed an apology was in order, but he didn't feel like it enough to stop them from leaving. He knew they had gone out of their way to help, but at the same time, they were just taking over and managing his life and he didn't like to be managed. He could do all right on his own.

Ru climbed the stairs slowly and went to his room where the little niche he had been given made him feel like he was more like an intruder. Ru sat down on the edge of the bed. It wasn't his bed. Those were not pictures he would choose to have on the wall. It wasn't his home and never would be. No doors were locked, to be sure, and yet he felt imprisoned in someone else's world. He wanted to be in his own world. 'This can't go on,' he said to himself. 'I have to think up something to do about it.'

CHAPTER FIVE

Solution?

RU SKIPPED SCHOOL ON MONDAY. HE WASN'T IN ANY MOOD TO FACE anyone at school. He hung around in the Mall all day, making sure he wouldn't go anywhere his uncle would find out about it.

That night he had the TV on in his upstairs room but wasn't actually looking at it. He was too busy thinking, building the case for how he could get out of the fix he was in. He figured that if he went back home, his uncle and aunt would just come out and insist that he come back here. *'Maybe if I did enough things that were bad enough, they would leave me alone,'* he reasoned in his desperate way. The idea of skipping out and hitch-hiking to somewhere far away pushed into his thoughts. *'Maybe I could get a good job where no one would know who I really am.'* This sense of being free from his present situation at his aunt and uncle's house, satisfied something in him that made it seem like that was the best thing he had thought of yet.

Ru didn't go to school again. Hiding out in the wooded area of a park all day, stretched out into his being glad when it would be time to go back to his uncle and aunt's place, as though he were just coming in after school. Right now, he was hungry, and could see the golden arches of McDonald's. Ideas were surging in his mind, *'I could get a burger and a drink and come back to my hideout.'*

After eating his burger, Ru decided to go up to the mall and walk around inside. When he went into a big department store, he looked around casually. But when he saw the blue jeans stacked on the shelves, two ideas came rushing together; *he could lift a pair and find a plaid shirt and when he got back to his uncle and aunt's place, and they wanted to know where he got them, he would just tell them, plain out, 'I stole them.' Maybe that would be doing something bad enough, they would wash their hands of me. Maybe that's when they would explode and say, 'That's it. We're through. You aren't going to stay here another day. Pack your things. We are going to take you back to your place and after that we don't care what happens to you. You don't care, so why should we care?'* Ru suddenly remembered the old story he heard in the fifth grade about the rabbit being thrown into the briar patch as punishment, when actually there wasn't any other place a rabbit would rather be.

Ru stuffed a pair of jeans under his jacket and then went over to look for a shirt the right size. When he found the right size shirt, he quickly stuffed it under the other side of his jacket and started for the door, looking around and thinking that nobody had seen him lifting the items. Less than a dozen steps outside the store, two men walked up beside him, one each side. One of them said immediately, "You better come with us."

As they walked back through the store, Ru realized it was the cameras. He knew most stores had them located all over the place.

In the security room, he was asked to show what he had in his jacket. He pulled the items out and said nothing. There was nothing to say. After asking him a lot of questions, one of the men reached over and picked up the phone and dialed the police department.

Down at the station, he had to tell them where he was living and why he wasn't in school. Defending his case, he told the whole story. That's when they called his uncle. After that, they explained the usual procedure. "You will get a hearing before the juvenile court. There's a good chance you will be sent to the Juvenile Center. Chances are they'll keep you there for evaluation. And don't take that the wrong way. Your offense is not all that bad, but it does seem like you need some time to back off and look at your life."

Aunt Mertie was with Uncle Hale when they came to the station and were told that there would be a hearing tomorrow morning, and that it's likely the juvenile judge will send him to the Juvenile Center. "He does that a lot," one of the officers said. Hale didn't object to the idea.

When the officer turned away to do some writing, Hale addressed Ru accusingly, "I don't see how someone who has been given the chance that we have given you could blow it so quickly and waste the opportunity. You need to be locked up somewhere!"

"He will stay here tonight," the officer said, when he returned. "Tomorrow morning a judge will have a hearing and decide what happens." He turned to Ru's uncle and aunt and said, "We will expect you to be here at nine o'clock."

"We'll be here," Hale said in a tone of closure. "What he needs is somebody who can turn his life around. We tried. But, he doesn't seem to know what an opportunity looks like."

Mertie couldn't help but put in her two cents worth as she

spoke to the officer. "I just don't understand that boy. You send him off to school in the morning and the next thing you know he's in jail."

Turning toward Mertie, Hale continued the accusation. "Well, it's obvious. He's just like his mother and daddy. Both of them failed him. I don't care if his mother is your sister, you'll have to admit that she failed him - running off with that man from Texas. And his Pa - what he liked was his drink. And now, when we try to help, all he cares about is fighting, drinking and stealing. You'd think he would have more respect for us than to do what he has done. He needs to get a taste of what it's like to pay for doing wrong. Let him stay in jail, or whatever." Turning back to the officer, who had just been sitting there listening, Hale said, "We'll be here tomorrow, but after that, we're through with him."

Hale was getting his feelings off his chest, but by this time, his Aunt Mertie was beginning to feel sympathetic. "That's no way to talk about your nephew," Mertie said. "It's not all his fault. He's had so many strikes against him. And it will be just one more strike against him if we turn our backs now. I'm not taking up for my sister - running off from home and leaving him alone with his drinking daddy, but that doesn't make any difference. Ru is still part of the family and the least we can do is stand by him a little more."

"You can if you want to," Hale said. "I'm through."

Ru sat there hearing to their accusations. What they had said was not spoken to him but said so he would hear what was said. He felt anger, hurt, sadness, and so alone.

At the court the next morning, the juvenile justice judge listened to the summation, then made the sentence. "Six months in the Juvenile Center. That's what the center is for," he said, closing the file and placing it in front of him.

What followed was a speech. Or was it a sermon? Strangely, it didn't sound like either. There was a tone of compassion in the judge's voice, as he said, "There are no previous records against you, Ruben. What you did may have been only a foolish action on your part. But from here on, you don't have to follow that same kind of disrespect for the rules of society. You can easily turn old endings into new beginnings. Whether or not you will do that and become a good citizen is not something I can choose for you. You, and you alone, can decide that. What we know is that some people who get into trouble, learn from it and change, then turn out well. So, Ruben, I am going to send you to one of our correctional institutions for young people, where you will have a chance to demonstrate your determination to make the future better. You will be in their charge completely and will not be released for six months, or until they determine. It may be as much as a year. That will depend on how well you do. What I know is that there is always a good tomorrow beyond a bad yesterday. How do I know? I have traveled that road. There are surprising new beginnings beyond old endings. Maybe you can turn this into a good new beginning. It's up to you and what you make of it."

There was an awkward moment immediately after the judge stopped talking. Ru didn't know whether it was over, or not. His aunt seemed equally unsure, but not his Uncle Hale. He just got up and walked out. The judge picked up a sheet of paper, signed it and handed it to an officer and said to Ruben, "You can follow her."

Out in the corridor, another officer fell in stride with them and said, "We'll keep Ruben in jail here until arrangements can be made for taking him to the Juvenile Center.

At nine o'clock, a probation officer from the Juvenile Center came to get Ruben. The drive out to the center was new territory for Ru. The mountains showed the early touch of color, now that the leaves had been touched with a light frost. Looking at them seemed to be a way of indicating that neither of them was expected to talk. As for Ru, he didn't feel like talking.

They turned off the highway onto a smaller road that led out through a mountain valley. "Here we are," the driver said, as he turned into what seemed like a gate, only there was no gate across the road. Trees and shrubbery lined the drive as they went up to a long white building. They got out of the van in the parking lot, and started up the walkway to the building. Several kids were standing in a line at the front of the building. Some seemed younger, but some about his own age, and Ru guessed they were offenders like himself. It just didn't seem like he thought it would be - not like a wire-fenced prison he had seen once, with barbed wire on top of the fence.

Ru walked with the probation office into an office where the officer handed a folder to the receptionist. She looked inside the folder briefly, then stood and said, "Welcome, Ruben. Let me go in with you to Mr. Vale's office." With a very kind and pleasant voice she said, "Mr. Vale, I have a new young man for you." As she handed the file to him she said, " He is Ruben Dallin. But I see from his file that mostly he goes by Ru."

"Good morning, Ru," the director said, standing and extending his hand for a handshake. "I am Harding Vale." Ru hadn't expected the handshake and extended a rather limp hand as he responded with an awkward and unenthusiastic, "Good morning."

"Come on in, Ru, and have a seat here at the desk." Mr. Vale walked out with the receptionist and probation officer and talked a moment before he came back in.

Ru didn't know what to expect. So far it was different. Even so, he felt sheepish and nervous. He dreaded the talk that might be coming from this man who was six feet tall and weighed around two hundred pounds. His gold and brown plaid sport coat and tan slacks made him seem approachable, but still Ru expected to hear sternly about the rules he would have to obey. He couldn't figure out the handshake and being asked to have a seat at the desk. It seemed more like a business transaction was about to take place. When he had been taken to the police station, nobody had ever invited him to sit down at a desk, just at a plain gray table. But most of the time, he had remained standing, anxiously waiting before being ushered from one place to another, and finally into a jail cell. As he waited, he felt some sense of relief that he was just sitting in an office.

When Mr. Vale returned and sat down at his desk, then leaned back in a relaxed manner and said, "Ru, I am sure all this seems a bit strange right now, but relax and realize that all of us here are your friends. You'll learn a lot about this place in the next few months. At first everything and everybody will be new to you, but then you will get to know the program and the people here. The staff here is committed to being your friend and helping you build a future you can be proud to call your own.

You will have a cottage parent who will be able to tell you about the details of the program and the various routines that are a part of the training. Right now, I want you to meet the director of cottage life, and let him introduce you to your cottage parent who will then take you to your cottage."

Ru got up and followed Mr. Vale across the hall where he was introduced to Steve Watson. Once again he found himself seated across a desk and listening to an explanation of the program. Mr. Watson was a smaller man than Mr. Vale and had a beard. Ru was able to relax a bit more now as he listened.

Five minutes later they were on their way down a long corridor to the cottage where he was to stay, led by Carlos Gates, his cottage parent, who had come up to meet Ru and take him to his room. As they walked along, Carlos said, "There are lots of corridors and you may feel like you are always marching off to some place. While it may seem very mechanical, always to be marching, that's the way you get to the places that are important to your life here - from the dorm rooms, to the cafeteria, to the exercise room, to the classrooms, even to the detention rooms, should you ever need to be sent there, or even to the Quiet House. Hopefully, that won't be necessary. But day after day, you will hear the sound of footsteps on these long corridors. And you may remember hearing them years later, like a lingering echo. They are a part of your story. Yes, everybody has a story and right now this is a part of your story. But, Ru, let me assure you, it can be a part of something good, if you choose to make it that. That's what all of us are here for - to make something good happen in your story."

Ru followed Carlos on down the corridor and turned in to the Wilson cottage. "This is your cottage and your room will be room number four, down on the right. You will have a roommate. Your bed will be on the left. You will note that the pillow is neatly in place and the blanket carefully folded and laid across the foot of the bed. You will have your own small dresser. That's it. That's your space. The bathroom is on down the way. The recreation room is where you will have some free time, and where, for two hours a day, the television will be on. You can meet with other guys there, talk, play cards, table games, or even ping pong."

Activities like that were going on as they walked into the recreation room. The other boys looked up from their activities briefly, and then went back to what they were doing. Having a new boy come in was nothing new. They just knew that sooner or later all of them come and go, replaced by others.

"Listen up." Carlos called to the boys. "This is Ru Dallin. He will be in room four, with Larry. Soon as he gets packed in, you can get to know him."

"Ru," Carlos said, explaining, "I will be leaving at five. Then Hank Lawrence will be your cottage parent until one AM. Then Eric Sawyer will be with you until I get back tomorrow. I have told you the first names of your cottage parents. But you will always call them by their last name, preceded by, mister. So, welcome to the Wilson Cottage."

"Where you from, Ru?" Monty called from a game table.

"I am from Jonas Ridge." Ru said.

"I'm from Jonas Ridge, too," another boy said loudly from across the large room.

"Aw, shut up, Donnie," came an immediate response. "You ain't either. You are from nowhere."

"Shut up yourself, Monty. I come from a lot better place than you."

"What's your real name?" Donnie asked.

"My name is Ruben. But most people, where I grew up, just shortened it to Ru."

"You'll soon get to know these boys really well," Carlos said. "Come on, and I'll show you to your room where you can unpack your things, and then I'll show you a place down the hall where you can put your suitcase. Then just mingle. You will go to dinner soon after Mr. Lawrence comes in."

As Ru unpacked his things, it was obvious the clothes his aunt had packed for him were different from what most of the guys were wearing. They had on jeans and a tee shirt. His clothes were too nice and he would have been glad to have jeans and a shirt, like the ones he had stolen, but the store had kept them. He hoped the rest of the guys wouldn't make fun of his nicer clothes.

Mr. Lawrence came in and met Ru. In the recreation room, he said, "Okay, guys. Line up for dinner. And listen, Joey Macy, let's not have any more of talking in line like you did yesterday."

"Yes, sir," Joey said. "but tell Barco to quit stopping in front of me when the line hasn't stopped," Joey added.

"Ru, you can drop in at the end of the line for right now," Mr. Lawrence said. "Later I will give you a place in line, and then each time we line up you will be expected to be in that place. Okay?"

Ru didn't like the idea of lining up. It rubbed him the wrong way and made him feel like he was being treated like a little boy. But that didn't make any difference. Any time they went anywhere, they were in line. Waiting in line was just part of it, too. If another cottage was already going through the cafeteria line, your group had to wait until they got all the way down the chow line before your group could start. It was the same way after a meal - only one group got up and carried their trays to the clean-up window at a time. It was so boring to stand in line and wait. No wonder they picked at each other, if they thought they could get by with it.

When they got back to their cottage from dinner, they were free to do pretty much as they pleased. His roommate, Larry, showed him how his bed had to be made in the mornings, and what his duties would be in keeping the place clean.

There was no doubt that some of the boys were testing his tolerance by things they said. One boy made fun of where he was from. "Jonas Ridge," he said. "Nobody's ever heard of such a place. You sure you're not just making it up?"

Ru had to push down on his feelings just to let it alone. Ru was not the type to make a lot of noise and tended to keep to himself a lot. The other guys often took this outward quietness to mean they could run over him. One boy soon found it wasn't quite that easy.

When Ru came from the recreation room into his eight by ten room that he shared with Larry, he saw that someone had pulled his sheets down and ruffled his blanket until it looked like it had never been made up at all.

"Did you do that?" he said to Larry, as he was sitting on the side of his own bed.

"No," Larry said. "I didn't have a thing to do with it."

"Who did it?"

Larry didn't say a word or even move.

"I said, 'Who did it?'" Ru demanded sternly.

"You think I am going to tell? I ain't gonna put no mouth on somebody else."

Ru reached for Larry's cover and pulled the sheet down as far as he could. "You are going to tell me or else there won't be anything left of your bed."

"All right. Quit tearing up my bed. I'll tell you. I don't want any points on me. It was old Pete over there," he said, pointing across the hall.

Quick as a flash, Ru dashed across the hall and began jerking the cover off Pete's bed.

"Hey, Pete," someone yelled from the hall. "You better come up here. That new boy just tore up your bed."

Ru had hardly turned around to leave Pete's room when Pete came tearing up to his room and made straight for Ru.

Ru stepped to one side just in time to give Pete a shove that landed him on his own bed. Pete hadn't expected that, but he was back on his feet instantly and heading for Ru again. He came at Ru with such a force that he knocked him back across the hall and on Larry's bed.

"Get off my bed, you damn son of a bitch," Larry cursed.

Ru jumped up quickly and headed for Pete and took a big swing at him. He missed. But then, he took a step closer, and landed a right punch into Pete's jaw, then came up immediately under his chin with a left hook. He was ready to hit him again when he felt a big pull on his shoulder. With a quick look around, he realized it was the cottage parent. Ru stopped. "This sure is a poor way to start off your first day in here," Mr. Lawrence said, "You needn't think you can fight around here and make it any easier for yourself. Who started this, anyway?"

Pete answered defensively. "I was out in the recreation room when somebody told me to come back here, cause the new guy was tearing up my bed. He was pulling the cover off and putting it on the floor when I just walked in."

"Walked in?" the cottage parent said.

"Well, anyway he was tearing up my bed," Pete said. "You expect me to just take it, and let him get away with it because he is new?"

Ru watched the expression on Mr. Lawrence's face as Pete argued in angry defense, "It's the new boy's fault," Pete argued, in angry defense. "He started the whole thing."

Without answering back, Ru stepped across the hall into his own room and started making his bed again, still burning with resentment at every fold of the blanket. Mr. Lawrence stood in the door of Pete's room and began addressing him directly. "Okay, Pete. I'm sending a request for you to talk to the director of cottage life and I am not so sure but what you won't end up in the Quiet House. This is the third time this week you've been in a fight. You can't just keep on pushing your weight around this way. A few days in the Quiet House might teach you."

Maybe it was because Ru was new, but Mr. Lawrence didn't accuse him and tell him that he also would have to go see the cottage director. But it made him know for sure that he didn't like this place - that he had to find a way out. He longed to be back in the hills surrounding his little mountain house in Jonas Ridge. It just barely met the necessities of living but at least it was his, and would be far better than this. He had already heard some of the boys talking about one boy who ran and hadn't been found yet. Whether that was true, or just a bunch of wishful thinking, didn't matter. It made Ru begin to think about finding a way out, even if it took a desperate move.

Later in the afternoon, it dawned on him. *When he had taken his suitcase down to a storage room where they kept old tables and chairs, he remembered there was a window there that didn't look like it was locked very well, maybe never been locked well enough. At least it didn't look very secure when he had seen it. Just one distraction, and he could be down there and out the window before anyone knew he was gone.*

Ru waited and watched. There was an argument at the ping pong table. Everybody in the recreation room gathered around to hear the back and forth cursing and accusing, and maybe a fight. Ru decided this might be enough. He put on his jacket, slipped down the hall and was out the window in moments. He dropped down to the ground and began running for the steam plant. He turned the corner and headed for an old railroad car just sitting on the tracks. He went behind it quickly, looked around the corner, then made a dash for the woods and didn't look back until he was in the woods. On the other side of the woods, he waited until there were no cars coming, then dashed across the highway and slid down a bank into the underbrush. Soon he was following a creek through the undergrowth. At a bridge he climbed up the bank and watched. There was little traffic so he began to follow the road. Then, deciding that was too much risk, he left the road and climbed up a steep hillside to the crest of a ridge. When he came to a small clearing he dropped down, panting and exhausted. When he looked out over the valley he could see the Juvenile Center. The sudden sound of rustling leaves made him turn nervously and look, only to see a squirrel. He could feel the goose bumps going back down on his skin. There was no sign that he was being followed so he dropped back on the leaves to rest.

Moments later he opened his eyes to look up through the trees. The leaves were beginning to turn yellow and red. A few of them fluttered to the ground. Clouds moved across the sky like sailing ships.

It was no time for watching the clouds. He pulled to his feet and started climbing higher. At some places it was so steep he could barely get up without slipping back as much as he climbed up. Holding to small trees enabled him to climb faster. Once he got to the top of the steep hill he turned and surveyed the whole valley below. Not far from the Juvenile Center was a little white church which reminded him of the church where the funeral service for his Pa had been. And like the church at Jonas Ridge, the cemetery was just slightly up the hill. Seeing that little white church made him remember the at-home feelings he had grown up with in Jonas Ridge. It was a moment of resolve that no matter what it took he would get back there.

As darkness began to settle across the hills, the evening air became cold. He was still panting with each breath as he made his way among the trees. The sun tipped the peaks of the mountains and its shadows made the valley below dark and mysterious. The deep blue of the mountainside and the purplish gray of yet another peak farther away added to the sense that he was far away.

As the evening turned into night, he could see the lights of a car inching along the winding roads below. He decided to take a chance and go down and walk on the road. He could make a dash for the side of the road as soon as he saw the dimmest light approaching. Fewer and fewer cars were passing by now, but each time one approached his heart beat faster and he clamored for the brush and trees. Each time he wondered if it could be someone from the Juvenile Center, hot on his trail. It was no fun, but when he reached home it would all be worth it.

Ru judged that it was past midnight by the time he reached

lower elevations where straighter roads led down the valley toward Jonas Ridge. The shoes his aunt had bought for him were not good for mountain climbing and walking. His feet hurt. Every passing car was a nightmare, and he quickly made for whatever cover he could find, then felt a big relief when he saw the red of the taillights as they dimmed in the distance.

He was hungry, but not thirsty. He had taken care of that by getting down on his hands and knees and drinking from the mountain stream that the road followed. In the approach of dim daylight, he saw an apple orchard and climbed up the hillside and loaded his pockets with big juicy apples. It was enough to keep him going. Stopping was not an option.

Biting into the luscious apples didn't just satisfy his appetite, it made him even more sure he was ready to get back to the apple orchards in Jonas Ridge. He threw the apple core away and pulled another apple out of his jacket pocket. He sat down to rest as he munched on the apple, wishing he could sleep, but knew he had a good ways to go yet and had to keep pushing on.

He was close enough now, that, in the dim light of dawn, he could see the apple orchard on the hillside behind his house and on up from there to where they had been cutting trees when his Pa met his tragic death. Tears filled his eyes and he swallowed hard as he ran that scene in his mind. It had been so exciting to begin to work in a partnership with his Pa that had turned so quickly into tragedy. The one thought that kept surging through his mind was that he could take up the dream and carry it forward. Suddenly he felt a surging sense of anger that he had allowed his uncle and aunt to pull him away from his dream. He wished he had just refused to go. Nothing had gone right since then.

It was getting lighter now and he knew that if he was going to be home before full sunlight, he had to push on. He walked faster and hoped no one would see him. It wasn't long before he got to the dirt road that led up past his house and made a dash for the barn.

CHAPTER SIX

Almost Home

JUNE HYLAND CLIMBED TO THE TOP OF THE HILL BEHIND HER HOUSE and walked along the ridge at the edge of the apple orchard where her father, and three men, he had hired, were picking apples. Every evening after school she took her place along with them in what seemed a never ending task of getting the apple crop picked and in storage. Her sisters had helped in that annual effort before they got married and moved away.

She hummed a tune as she marched up the hill, munching on her usual after-school peanut butter and jelly sandwich. The orchard where they were picking today, was just down the slope from the top of the ridge. She was just about to turn to go down the slope when she saw someone make a dash into the barn of the Dallin place. Quickly she moved over so she could see the barn better. At first she thought someone might be stealing things, but as she held that glimpse in her mind she began to realize that it looked like Ru. And yet, she could not figure it out. She knew Ru

55

was in some kind of training school. She hadn't heard from him and wasn't even sure about that. She liked Ru and remembered how they had played together as children and sledded in the snow down these very slopes between the apple trees. He hadn't been a serious student and was ready to drop out of school. Then his Pa got killed in a tragic logging accident. June kept watching. It looked just like Ru. She decided to go closer.

Going on down the hill slowly, she got close to the edge of the grown-up orchard that Ru's granddad had nurtured so faithfully for so many years. June stood behind a tree among the weeds and watched. Whoever had gone into the barn had pulled the big sliding door back, leaving only a small crack. She knew someone had gone in there but wasn't about to go down and find out unless she was surer that it was Ru. She thought maybe she should go and tell her dad. Then she saw someone just barely looking out. The door opened wider. It was Ru all right. He must have run away from that training school, June concluded.

Her heart beat rapidly when she saw Ru dash out of the barn, cross the road and start up her way. But he stopped at an old apple tree, climbed up far enough that he could reach a few of the apples still growing on a tree where many of the limbs were dead. After he had stuffed a few apples in his jacket, and jumped down and started racing for the barn, June decided to make herself known.

"Hey, Ru," she called.

Ru kept running toward the barn and dashed inside. Either he hadn't heard her or hadn't recognized her. In any case, he kept running like he was scared.

June walked out to the edge of the orchard and paused. She called out again. "Ru. It's me. June."

There was no reply but Ru stepped out just far enough to wave his arm and motion for her to come down there.

"Quick. Come in here," Ru said.

As soon as they were inside Ru pulled the old barn door closed again. "Did anyone see you come down here?" he asked anxiously.

"No. I don't think so," June answered.

"I need to know for sure," Ru said. "Are you alone?"

"I'm alone," June said. "But what are you doing here? I thought you had gone off to live with your uncle and aunt and to go back to school."

Ru took a big bite of his apple and chewed it just enough so he could talk. "That's right. But I couldn't stand their world. Got in trouble and ended up in the Juvenile Center. June, you won't tell anyone I'm here, will you?" They will come for me from the center if they know I am here. They will come to the house first thing."

"Won't they come out here, too, if they think you are anywhere around? Being out here in the barn is no better than being in the house."

"I guess so," Ru answered. "But I figure I can keep a good lookout. Then if they come up here I have bales of hay fixed so I have a little room in there and can pull a bale over the entrance and they will never know I'm in there. I fixed it as soon as I got here this morning."

"But it's cold out here, Ru," June said compassionately. "You'll freeze to death on cold nights. You can't stay out here."

"It won't be too bad," Ru answered, "once I get into my little room in the hay."

"But how will you live? You can't stay out here all the time. And you can't live on apples."

"I know," Ru admitted. "But I can't live where I was, either. I can't stand that place. I'll starve before I go back."

"Is it all that bad?" June asked. "Don't they feed you well?"

"Oh, I guess so, but I don't like being cooped up in somebody else's world and treated like I am nobody."

"Ru, I don't have time to listen now, June said. "I have to go. I'm supposed to be helping Dad pick apples. He'll be wondering about me." June started for the door.

Ru walked over to open the door, but before he pulled on it he paused and ventured a question. "June, I know this is asking a lot, but do you think you could bring me something to eat?" He was looking into her brown eyes and almost pleading. "I don't have any money or I'd ask you to go down to the store and buy me something."

The eyes of childhood playmates were sharing a moment of unbroken devotion as June looked into Ru's face. "Sure, Ru. I'll find some way to get you something besides apples."

"But don't bring it till almost dark. Somebody might see you." Ru asked.

"Okay," June agreed and slipped through the opening in the door after Ru had looked both ways and decided it was clear.

Ru watched as June made her way quickly up into the orchard. He realized she was no longer just the childhood friend he had known, or just a classmate. She was somebody he admired. To him she was beautiful, in her jeans, yellow blouse and blue sweater. He watched until she disappeared among the apple trees.

The next morning, June sat on a bale of hay and watched Ru devour the food she had sneaked out for him before going to school. "Ru, I can't keep this up. I can't keep making up excuses to leave the house right after supper, and then going to school early." June argued.

"I know, June. And I can't blame you. I don't want you to get into trouble. Reckon what your dad would say if he knew what you are doing?"

"I don't know, but I know he'd be plenty mad if I lied to him, and he found out about that. That's one thing he expects - absolute honesty. I've heard him say it many times. In fact, I've heard him say that enough, that I know I'm being dishonest just doing what I am doing, even if he knows nothing about it."

"Do you think he'd turn me in if he knew I am here?" Ru pressed. "Do you think he'd let me stay out here?"

"I don't know, Ru. But I think he'd say that knowing you are here and hiding is a form of dishonesty in itself. You know Dad enough to know that's how he is." June responded intensely.

Ru surprised June when he said, "I want you to tell him I'm here. I want you to tell him when I came, and why. Tell him that Uncle Hale and Aunt Mertie pressured me to leave here in the first place. Tell him that it just didn't work out at their house. They wanted to protect me but all they did was control my life. Dressed me like a city boy. Put me in a school where I didn't fit. And, yes, tell him that I got into trouble there and got sent to the Juvenile Center. I don't belong in the center. I belong out here. Pa and I were going to turn this farm into a success, then he got killed. I know you need to go, June, but will you explain it to your dad?"

"I will, Ru. I'll tell him later this evening, if that's what you really want," June said kindly.

"I think so. I know I can't stay out here like this. And, thank you, June, for being so nice to me." Ru reached out and took her hand to help her up from where she was sitting on the bale of hay. Almost to his own surprise, he didn't let go of her hand when they were both standing. He had perhaps taken her hand many times when they played as children, but this time it was different. He had a special feeling for her. June must have felt it, too, for she didn't pull her hand away. They looked at each other in a way that each of them must have known what the other one was feeling. Ru let go of her hand and they both climbed down the ladder. They were close to each other when they got to the big barn door. Ru was about to open the door when he looked at June. She was already looking at him and into his eyes. Ru reached down for her hand and squeezed it gently. She returned the gentle touch. Still holding her hand, Ru slipped his arm around her and placed a kiss on her waiting lips. Surprise showed in both their faces as they pulled away enough to see into each other's expression. For a moment they just stood there smiling at each other in the rapture of their new discovery. Knowing that she really had to go, Ru pulled the door open and looked all around. He held her hand as she slipped through the door and then slipped away into the dusk of early evening.

Ru was about to make his way back into his hiding place when he heard a car and saw lights coming up the road. He climbed up into the barn loft quickly and watched through the cracks. His heart was beating rapidly. Quickly he grabbed the few apples still lying on a bale of hay and stuffed them in the hay. He looked out again and saw the car creeping along in front of his house. The car stopped. Two men got out and went up to the house. One of them tested the door and found it was locked. After he came back down the old steps, both of them walked around the outside of the house and then came back to the van. When they both got back in they drove out to the barn. The lights were shining full blast at the barn.

Ru climbed into his little niche in the hay and made himself comfortable in a sitting position, and reached over and pulled the bale of hay so it closed the entrance. He wondered if he had left anything outside as a clue. The van doors slammed and he heard the old barn doors roll back. He knew they were inside. Flashlights beamed in all directions. One man climbed up the ladder to the barn loft and shined the light all around up there and slowly climbed back down. "There's nobody here," he said. "No telling where that kid is. He may be in another state by this time." Ru didn't hear them pull the barn door back together, but then he heard both doors of the van slam closed. Ru breathed a sign of relief and pushed the hay bale slightly open just enough that he could see through the cracks and see the red lights of the van as it turned around and then faded into the darkness.

Ru was ready to crawl back into his little hay room and snuggle down for the night when he saw lights coming up the road again. The chill of fear rushed back into his whole body as he wondered if they had turned around and decided to take another look. The car didn't stop at the house this time but drove right up to the barn. Just when Ru was pulling the bale of hay over the little entrance to make sure he was hidden, he realized it didn't sound like the van when the doors opened and went closed again.

"Ru," a girl's voice called out. "Ru, it's June. We're coming in."

Ru took a deep breath of relief. He pushed the bale of straw aside and climbed out of his hiding. The beam of light from a flashlight blinded his eyes, but not so much but what he could see that it was John Hyland, climbing up the ladder.

"Come on out, Ru," John said, and turned the light away so he wouldn't be blinded by it.

Ru climbed over the bale of hay, brushed himself off and followed Mr. Hyland down the ladder. When they both were down, Mr. Hyland didn't say anything but reached around Ru's shoulder and gave it a strong and fatherly hug. They followed June as she led the way out the barn door "Let's go over to the house," Mr. Hyland said. Ru closed the barn door behind them.

"I bet you are about half frozen," John Hyland said. "The car is warm. Get in and lets go to the house and get warmed up. You're shaking like a leaf."

"Only some of that comes from being cold." Ru said. "The rest comes from being scared. When you drove up, I was almost sure it was someone from the center making one more search around. So, was I ever glad when I heard June call my name."

Walking into the warm and lighted house was like heaven to Ru after spending the night before in the cold barn. He'd had enough of his own imprisonment.

Ru backed up to the stove in the den, then turned and held his hands out over the stove. "Go wash your hands, Ru," Mrs. Hyland said from the kitchen. "Get ready to eat a hot meal. I know you must be hungry."

Whatever June had told her parents it must have been received with kindness. Sitting down at the table made Ru feel like a king. He could hardly wait to begin eating. Mr. Hyland sat down at the end of the table, turning slightly sideways as he sipped his coffee. Ru sat down at the other end where there was a place set for him.

June sat over on the side of the table. "The bread is hot," Mrs. Hyland said. "And so are the eggs and ham and gravy. Dig in, Ru. Welcome back. And would you like some hot coffee, too?"

Ru wasn't used to drinking coffee but he said, "That would be fine."

June was not sitting right up at the table, but moved closer to the table when Mr. Hyland said, "Perhaps we should say a prayer of thanks." Folding his hands on the edge of the table, he offered a simple prayer of thanks. The resonant voice in the prayer was one that he heard before when he had eaten there as June's playmate. Tonight it sounded even more kind and sincere. As soon as Mr. Hyland said, 'Amen', he leaned back, took up his coffee cup and said, "Make yourself at home, Ru. Eat all you want. It's good to have you here."

Ru was too hungry to do anything else. He knew he had never tasted better ham and eggs, biscuits and gravy. After that, he relished blackberry jelly and biscuits. At Mrs. Hyland's insistence, he took out a second biscuit, pulled it open and covered it with jelly. Ru had barely tasted the coffee, but Mrs. Hyland filled the cup again and poured herself a cup and sat down across from June.

It was the only real freedom Ru had known since the day he left Jonas Ridge. He knew the atmosphere in this home was real and not a put-on. John and Marie Hyland were known all over the valley as some of the best people one could ever know. This special moment confirmed all of that for Ru.

A silence fell on their conversation and Ru felt it was his time to say something. But before he could begin, Mr. Hyland said, "Ru, what are you going to do?"

It was the question Ru had rolled over in his mind again and again, especially since he had asked June to tell Mr. Hyland that he was back in Jonas Ridge.

"Do you think I could go back on my own?" Ru asked.

Mr. Hyland did not answer quickly. "I believe in being totally honest," he said. "And I believe every problem has a solution and a good one if we try to make it that."

Ru knew Mr. Hyland was giving him a chance to make his own decision. "That means I should go back, doesn't it?" Ru said in a question response. He already knew what the answer to the question needed to be, but he wanted to hear Mr. Hyland say it.

"I couldn't keep you here and be honest," Mr. Hyland answered. "I am sure I can count on you to do the right thing."

"I'll go back," Ru said decisively.

Spending the night and having breakfast the next morning at the Hyland home was like a dream fast forwarding beyond the turmoil of the last few weeks. There was a sense of wholeness about the Hyland family Ru wished he could build into his own story in his future. He was ready to get started on that future.

Early that morning, Ru walked with June down to the school bus stop and said a reluctant goodbye as she got on. As Ru walked back up the road, he looked up at the little house where he had grown up. It seemed strangely like yesterday and tomorrow, like both an old ending and new beginning. He wondered if the new beginning that his Pa had made, that lasted only such a short time, could be extended in some way into his own story. That's when Ru thought of the book his father held in his hand that day he sat on the porch reading. Almost talking to himself, Ru resolved, '*I want that book.*' He walked quickly toward the house. Reaching for his billfold, and taking out the key he had tucked in one of the little pockets as a treasured link, he opened the door. The sounds were distinctly like yesterday as the door squeaked open. The book was on the table in the den beside the chair where his Pa sat most often. Somehow it represented his own tomorrow as he picked up the book and thumbed its pages, stopping on the last chapter, with the title, 'Turning Point'.

Ru tucked the book under his arm, reached in his pocket for the key and turned and locked the door back. Somehow that book seemed like another key in his hand to grasp a new future as he walked back up the road beside the creek to the Hyland home.

Ru waited in the den by the stove, still holding the book. "What's the book?" Mrs. Hyland asked, when she came in from the kitchen. Ru responded immediately. "It's the book my Pa was reading before he died. It's *NEW TOMORROWS*. I think it may have been what changed his own story. I can't wait to read it."

"Ready to go?" Mr. Hyland said as he came into the den.

"Ready to go!" Ru said.

CHAPTER SEVEN

Re-launch

THE RETURN TO THE JUVENILE CENTER WAS A RETURN TO THE OFFICE of Steve Watson, the Director of Cottage Life. Ru waited for the words he knew would come. They came, but not before Ru was greeted and asked to have a seat at the desk. Stern rebuke was what Ru expected, but what the director said was, "Ru, even though you came back on your own, which counts for a lot and is commendable, we have a standard procedure here. If a student goes on the runs, when we get him or her back, there are five days in the Quiet House. It's not punishment. It's re-launch. It's a time to look at your life and the story you are writing. In the Quiet House you will have the bare essentials and you'll be in seclusion. Your food will be brought to you. You will have only your underclothes and pajamas to wear. It'll be warm enough that you will not need a blanket. All you will have will be the essentials of a bathroom. You will have a mattress and a mattress pad. The lights will stay on day and night. There are no windows and you may not know if it's night or day. To borrow a term from the business world, it's a think tank, your own think tank, all by yourself.

We will give you some materials to read which are designed to help you think in a new direction."

"I already have something to read," Ru entered quickly.

"Well, we will give you what we want you to read," Steve Watson rebutted.

"But look at this book," Ru said, handing it across the desk. "I want to read this book while I am in there. It's one my Pa was reading before he died. A minister gave it to him. I want to see what it's about? Look at it and look at the title of the last chapter."

Turning through the pages to the beginning of the last chapter he read, "'Turning Point.' Okay. You may take that, also."

Isolation was what Ru wanted most for the next five days. Instead of drudgery, it seemed like a window, opening to a new understanding of himself in his windowless little world. Each of the ten stories and accompanying philosophy seemed like a promise from the future. Like the people in the stories, he saw himself being a winner now, on both his chosen and un-chosen journey.

Five days later, when Brian Valdosky opened the door and invited Ru out of the Quiet House, he noted the book Ru clutched in his hand like a treasure. Once they were seated across a desk from each other, the counselor asked about the book. "Is that what you have been reading? We expected you to read the material we gave you. Did you read that?"

"Oh, yes, sir. But I also read this book," Ru said, handing the book across the desk.

"That's interesting, and very coincidental," Mr. Valdosky said. "That's the book we are going to be using in a special set of classes here soon. Of course, we are not sure you will be here when the class is offered. But we'll see. The staff will have an evaluation session to determine where you go next. Sometimes those who run are sent to another correctional unit. They will decide.

"I'd like to be a part of any class in which that book is used," Ru cut in, almost in pleading tone.

"We'll see," Mr. Valdosky said, and stood up to turn Ru over to the cottage parent of a different cottage than the one he had been in previously. "In the meantime you will have a session with a psychologist, the nurse who saw you once a day while you were in the Quiet House, a social worker from the center, and then with the school principal. They will all be there when the evaluation committee meets to decide about where you will be sent. I'll be in the meeting and tell them about your treasured book, *NEW TOMORROWS*. In fact, I am going to get a copy for myself and read it before the evaluation session," he said, as he handed the book back to Ru.

Max Green, the Juvenile Center Administrator was already seated at the conference table, ready to lead the evaluation session, when Steve Watson, Director of Cottage Life, and Laura Finn came in. After a few minutes, Brian Valdosky came in with the school principal, Berton Andrews,

Sarah Morgan, social psychologist, came in late and was kidded, saying they had just voted for her to lead all the cases for placement today. She took the teasing in stride, and said, "I will take any case except the Sue Blevins case. I sometimes think she may be bipolar, and that one of the persons she lapses into just delights in making me, as her psychologist, look plain stupid."

The staff had worked together so much that there was a wholesome sense of camaraderie among them in which they often talked about the students as though they were like their own children.

Max Green opened the meeting on a light note saying, "Miss Morgan, did you say you wanted to take up the Sue Blevins case first?"

"Nooooo. That's not what I said at all," Sarah said, as she flipped her long blond hair behind her shoulder, "I think Ted Welch wants to bring up his case first." She looked at him in a jesting manner. "Isn't that right?"

"Well, that's not what I said, but I will bring up the first case, if that's okay." Ted shuffled a few pages and said, "Let's start with Ruben Dallin, from Jonas Ridge. At least that's where he grew up. He's sixteen now. His mother left home with a man from Texas and hasn't been seen since. His father had been a man of the bottle. Then he was killed in a logging accident a few months ago. Ruben went to live with his uncle and aunt and started in a new school. He got into fights and was arrested for being drunk at a ball game. After that he was arrested for stealing a pair of blue jeans and a shirt at a department store. That's when the juvenile judge sent him here. In only a few days he went on a run and went back to his home in Jonas Ridge. But he decided to give himself up and came back on his own."

Ted searched the papers in his folder. "What about his records at school? What is his IQ on the test you gave him, Miss Morgan?"

"Oh, his IQ is high enough. He scored above average, way above." She said. "But his school records do not match his IQ. Something must have happened."

"And what about his attitude? Has it changed?"

"Let me speak to that," Brian Valdosky interjected. "There's something special about this boy. He has a book that is very special to him, says it is one that his Pa read that changed his life. It's the one he brought back with him after he went on a run. It's the one he begged us to let him take into the Quiet Room. Unusual as it may seem, it's the very book that Judge Art Williams is going to be using in a course that is going to be offered here at the center. And you all know what Mr. Williams says - he says he gives the course because he wants to help young people who may be as far off track as he was when he was their age. So when Ruben, he refers to himself as Ru, when Ru learned about the course, he almost pleaded for the opportunity to be in that class. I said, "We'll see," knowing that he might not even stay here once this placement committee meets."

"Do you think he'll run again?" Miss Morgan asked Brian.

"From what I have learned about him, there's not a chance," Brian said. "And the reason I say that has to do with that book he treasures, called *NEW TOMORROWS*. I've read the book and it's not like any book I have ever read before. The granddad in the book reaches back into stories from the past, but tells them like they are a call from the future - new beginnings beyond old endings. In fact, that is the sub-title of the book. And if there is a chance he can be a part of Judge Williams' class, I think he ought to get that chance. So, to the question about whether he should be sent to another center, or stay here, I say, let's let him stay here."

"What do the rest of you think?" Max Green inquired, going around the room for responses.

"Stay here." was the recurring response.

"The consensus seems to be that you want to see what can

happen if he stays and is allowed to take Judge Williams class - perhaps stay here until graduation? Is that it?" Max Green summarized.

"Then he'll stay here?" Miss Morgan asked.

"Seems unanimous," Max Green responded. "Ru stays here.
Make sure he gets in Art Williams' class."

CHAPTER EIGHT

New Beginnings

AS SCHOOL PRINCIPAL, BERTON ANDREWS WARMLY INTRODUCED ART
Williams to the class of seven boys and five girls. "Our leader
for these classes we will have here each Wednesday is Judge Art
Williams. But more than being a judge before young people, Judge
Williams is a friend of young people. And Mr. Williams has been a
very special friend of the Juvenile Center and has given his classes
here six times. This is now the seventh time we have had the
privilege of having this distinguished leader and friend to young
people here to lead this class. So, now let's welcome Judge Williams
with a round of applause." The applause was timid, with students
wondering what a judge would say.

Judge Williams walked to the center of the classroom. After
placing a folder and a book on the table in a very relaxed manner,
he walked around to the front of the table and said, "I am Judge
Art Williams. You are probably already thinking, 'Here comes the
judge'. Well, you may be a bit surprised by this judge. You are not

going to get a lecture about how bad you are. That's not quite the way it's going to be. Instead, I am going to talk about change, and how good you can be. I am going to talk about the promise of the future in the greatest age the human family has ever known, about how you can turn old endings into new beginnings and turn your problems into opportunity.

Years ago I found my way to new beginnings. My interest in being here is to help you do the same. I once walked in your shoes. I had to put my own past behind me so I could put a new future before me. It was a choice that only I could make.

This is the seventh time I have come out to the Juvenile Center campus to give this short-term class. A lot of the students, like you, who have been in my classes, first got to know me when they stood before my bench and I had to hand down a sentence. Many times I assigned those young people to this place. Some of you here today may be among them."

'*That's it,*' Ru resolved in his mind, immediately, '*I thought he looked like someone I had seen. I remember it now. He's the one who sent me here.*'

"I didn't become a judge to hand out penalties. I became a judge to help young people like you draw a new picture of success, then never walk away from that picture, so that you never have to come before me, or any judge, again. Why? It's because when I was in your situation and your age, I stood before a judge who had a heart. Even when he represented the law, he was kind and caring. When I came up through the ranks as a lawyer and became a judge, I decided I was going to be that kind of judge. So, I have been a volunteer teacher out here for the past six spring sessions with the goal of helping young people see a new dream for themselves. Be assured that as I come for this seventh time, I come as your friend.

This year the class is going to be about tomorrow. It's going to be about ten words anyone can choose to define who he or she is, and can become.

I want to tell you where you can find those ten words. They are in a book with the engaging title, *NEW TOMORROWS. New Beginnings Beyond Old Endings for the Digital-Information-Molecular Age.* It's a book I treasure greatly. It's the book I hold in my hand. It has ten stories which are a backdrop on the past but define the future. They are stories about turning points - about turning failure upside down. Each of you will be given a copy of the book at the end of today's class.

What I have learned that is very interesting, is that one of you has already read this book. In fact, this student has read it twice. I learned that this person read it while in the Quiet House. You know about the Quiet House, don't you?"

A ripple of laughter followed from the twelve students in the classroom. Judge Williams had their full attention now. "Some learn about the Quiet House first hand. Others hope they would never have to learn about it. And you may be wondering who among you has read the book I am talking about."

Ru wasn't sure if he were the only one who had read the book, but he was pretty sure he was the only one who had read it twice.

"I don't mean to single anyone out without that person being willing to be known," Mr. Williams said. "But if you are the person who has read this book twice and is willing to let it be known, you can do so by raising your hand. You don't have to, but it's your chance to let your fellow students know how much you respect what the 'granddad' in the book has to say."

Ru didn't hesitate. He raised his hand immediately. He was proud to do so. The book had changed the way he saw the world and his place in it.

Judge Williams spoke directly to Ru and said, "I am glad you are willing to be known in this special way. What I wonder is if you would tell us how you came across this book and chose to read it. Do you mind, Ru? See, I already know your name, and in time I'll get to know each of you by name as we share our stories together. You are my new friends. So, Ru, if you choose to tell your story, you don't need to come up here. You can share your story from right where you are. I used the term 'right where you are' as a kind of metaphor that you will hear me use many times. Not somewhere else, but right here - right where you are - is a special moment and place in the story that each of you is writing."

Students turned toward Ru as he began. "I first learned about NEW TOMORROWS, when I saw my Pa reading it, sitting on the porch of our little mountain house. Pa didn't do much reading. In fact, I can't remember ever seeing him reading a book before that. He was more interested in a bottle than a book. But that book changed his life. After he read that book, his focus was on the future and on writing his own story as a new beginning beyond old endings. A 'New Beginnings Beyond Old Endings,' that's in the title of the book. I won't go into the rest of the story except to say that things went wrong in my life, and I got in so much trouble that I appeared before Judge Williams. And I was somebody who needed his own new beginning. Soon after I got here, I went on a run. While I was on that run I had a chance to go by my house and get the book my Pa had been reading. And when I got back here, and when they put me in the Quiet House, I asked if I could take the book with me in there. Some of you know what it's like in there, nothing much to do but eat, sleep, and think, and read, if you choose. I chose to read and so I read the book twice. And I am ready to read it again. I assume that's what Judge Williams will expect."

"You are right, Ru," Judge Williams said. "But it's not a requirement. It's a choice. In fact, the book itself is about the story you are writing and the choices you will make in the greatest age the world has ever known.

We live in the cell phone age. We can connect with people anywhere in the world in seconds just by pushing a few buttons. The only reason we have cell phones is because there has been a progression of knowledge from the time of Moses, and his ten words were chiseled on stone, up to our time of cell phones. I didn't even use a phone of any kind until I got to college. Yes, I grew up the hard way. Now, all of us have the benefits of what I call the progression of the human story. We are at a turning point in that story. There are ten words that can become guiding markers in our story. They are not religious words, just successful achievement words. They are markers anyone can choose to guide his or her success story.

They are simple, but basic. Here they are. KINDNESS. CARING. HONESTY. RESPECT. COLLABORTION. TOLERANCE. FAIRNESS. INTEGRITY. DIPLOMACY. NOBILITY. That's all. Just ten. I call them the Big Ten.

I often like to put them together in twos. Like, Kindness and Caring. Honesty and Respect. Collaboration and Tolerance. Fairness and Integrity. Diplomacy and Nobility. You can carry these words in your mind to guide your tomorrows so you can have a good and successful life. If you will let these ten words shape your identity and guide your story, you will like yourself more and find your best paybacks from life all across your years. It's like the "granddad" says in the book, what you plan to give to life becomes your request of life. So, you can afford to give your best dreams their best chance to happen; they become your request of life.

But let me warn you now. These ten words are tough. They are a challenge to live by. Or should I say, 'live up to,' for they define a new reach for the next level up. But nobody is going to make you live by them. They have to be chosen. And you are the chooser! Even though they are hard to live up to, they can help you be a better person and write your own success story as one you will be proud to call your own.

What I have done is to have those ten words printed on a card which will fit into your pocket or billfold. They are not so much something you will be showing to others, as your self-chosen identity words you can show to your own mind. Then someday you may want show them to other people and tell them that they were turning point words that helped you turn your way to a successful life of new beginnings.

What's important is that you keep showing these ten words to yourselves as a way of telling your mind who you want to be. If you show that ten-words-picture of yourself to your own mind, in turn, your mind will reset itself so that it guides you to find ways to become that new chosen person. And even if you never show them to anyone else, people will recognize the effect these ten positive words have had on your life - that you have been reaching up, beyond your failures for your next level up in your own success story. The words may be your secret identity. But, of course, the identity will leak out because you will be a better person just for letting these words be your identity markers.

As you leave the classroom, I want each of you to come by for your card and book. As you come by, I want to learn your name as the name of a new friend. And I want you to feel free to linger and talk to me and tell me any part of your story you want to share with me as your friend. That way we will be trying together to be Big Ten people."

When Ru came by, Judge Williams said, "Thank you, Ru, for letting the class know that you were the one who had read *NEW TOMORROWS*."

"I was glad to do it," Ru said. "And I am glad to be in your class. Thank you for coming out here to teach it."

The class, that met one time each week, was something Ru looked forward to eagerly. Beyond that he had now taken a new interest in school. Biology and chemistry were among his favorite subjects. They seemed to fit with what he would need to know once he graduated from high school at the Juvenile Center and got back to Jonas Ridge and started restoring the apple orchard. It was a dream that once seemed beyond reach, but included going to the nearby community college to study horticulture.

Judge Williams met with the class for ten successive weeks, by using one of the ten stories each week. In the last week, he held up the book and said, "One story in this book is about Joseph. His story had several new beginning points before he found his way to reach his dreams and to achieve a very special success. Even though you have already read Joseph's story in your book, I want to abbreviate that story and tell it, so you can hear it told by someone who knows the story as a kind of parallel passage. It's a story about not giving up. Joseph just wouldn't give up. Nor should you.

Things haven't gone right in your story or you wouldn't be here now. I was at that same point in my story at your age. I made some mistakes. Big ones. How did I find my way out of the pit? It was at a center like this where I had a friend who just wouldn't give up on me. I could tell you all about my pit story, but that wouldn't be worth as much as your hearing Joseph's story. So, let me tell you Joseph's success story.

CHAPTER NINE

The Joseph Dream Vision

JUDGE WILLIAMS STOOD BEFORE HIS TREASURED LITTLE CLASS, LOOK-
ing up and beyond the classroom as though he could imagine and
see far back in time.

"A grove of old olive trees surrounded the cluster of tents where
Jacob lived with his shepherd family. Fig bushes grew near the
spring. The desert winds rustled the flaps of the tent where Jacob
and his family gathered one morning for breakfast. Joseph was next
to the youngest of Jacob's twelve sons, and the one who bounced
in, plopped down on the carpet and began telling the dream he
just dreamed.

"We were all out in the field binding wheat into bundles. It was
so funny! The sheaf that represented me was just standing there,
and the sheaves which represented all of you were bending over
and bowing down to my sheaf. I am not sure I can explain such a
strange dream."

Quickly one of his brothers cut in with sarcasm and said, "I don't have any problem explaining it. You think you are better than the rest of us, especially when you wear that boastful multi-colored coat. So, you want to be king over us, is that it, dreamer boy? Well, eat your breakfast, grow up, and forget your dreams. Maybe we'll let you help us be shepherds." Scornful laughter from the other brothers erupted.

One day Joseph's father sent him out to find out where his brothers were tending the sheep. Joseph put on his special coat of many colors and set off to find his brothers.

Many dusty miles later, he climbed up on a steep, rocky hillside so he could see far away. Shading his eyes, he scanned the horizons until he saw them in the distance. He climbed back down the bluff and increased his pace across the sagebrush and sparsely grassed flatlands, filled with excitement to be on a mission of importance for his father, and eager to be one of the big brothers.

After many miles, he came upon their camp site. He had visions of their being so glad to see him they would come out to meet him. As he approached with hurried steps he called an exciting 'hell-looo!' But no one was rushing out to meet him. As he neared the tent he slowed his pace to a halting walk. Finally, he approached their glaring silence. "What's wrong?" he asked.

"What's wrong?" one brother countered quickly. "Guess you wouldn't know, would you, wearing a fancy coat like that out here in desert country? But maybe you came out here to become the chief shepherd and let us bow down to you, is that it, dreamer boy? Maybe you'd like to show us how. Go ahead. Bow down, dreamer boy. Show us how."

Joseph was only inching his way forward now, thinking they

might come and force him to his knees. They did approach, but instead of making him bow down, one of them grabbed him, and yanked off his precious coat. Then, after holding his coat up as an object of derision, his brother dropped it on the ground. Joseph reached down to get it, but his brother quickly put his foot on it and twisted it into the dirt.

Then other brothers came over, and two of them grabbed Joseph's arms and began pulling him away from the camp. Soon Joseph saw they were approaching a dry well, and had no doubt what they were planning to do. He began to resist with all his might, and plead, "Please don't throw me in there," but they gave him one final push and his resisting feet slipped over the side and he began bumping and scraping his way down to a stunning thud at the bottom of the pit.

Slowly, Joseph pulled himself up to a sitting position and leaned back against the walls of the pit. He listened. There were no sounds. He looked up from the darkness at the small circle of light above.

This was not a part of his dream. He had thought he would be looked up to by his brothers. Now he knew how much they looked down on him. How could he have been so foolish to believe in his dreams? Hadn't what just happened made a mockery of his dreams?

Joseph's brothers slowly made their way back to the camp and sat down. The only sounds to be heard were the shuffling movement and bleating of the sheep. Nobody said anything for a long while. Out of the stillness, Judah turned his head to one side. "Listen," he said. "What's that? Sounds like a bell."

They all listened. Judah stood up and walked in the direction from which the sound seemed to be coming. Amid a cloud of dust, he could see a line of camels, inching along the edge of a distant rocky hillside. "Come and look," he said. His brothers rushed over. The jingling sound of a bell became louder.

"It's a caravan of traders," one of the brothers said. "Let's go out and meet them and see what they have to sell."

"Better still," Judah said, "let's sell something to them."

"We don't have anything to sell that they want, unless they want some sheep," came the immediate reply.

"Who says we don't have anything to sell? I know one thing we could sell and they would pay a good price for it," Judah countered.

"What's that?" the brother quizzed quickly.

"A slave. A boy slave. Joseph. They'll pay good money for him."

"Well, what are we waiting for?" Simeon said. "Let's pull him up and take him to them."

"Not so fast," Judah said. 'Let's talk to them first. We can tell them we have something valuable they would like to see."

When the traders arrived at the edge of the pit, they were eager to see what the shepherds had to offer.

When a rope was thrown down to Joseph, he gladly took hold of it and began climbing out of the pit, thinking his brothers had changed their minds - that his dream was not ending after all.

But once Joseph was out of the pit and saw the traders, he knew it was a far different story. He was being sold by his own brothers. He watched in helpless disbelief as his brothers accepted twenty pieces of silver for him.

The traders tied Joseph's wrists together with a rope and then tied the other end of the rope to a pack on a camel. Joseph followed the caravan through the desert, in a daze of disbelief. As he trudged along, he looked back and saw his brothers huddled together and watching. Joseph lifted his tied hands, as best he could, to wave to his brothers. They didn't wave back. His homeland faded into the distance.

Joseph had been pulled out of the pit, but who would he be now that he was out? Would he live out a kind of extended reaction to that one painful event? Would he be angry, bitter, and defiant toward anyone who seemed to represent an extension of the pit and his brother's wrong? Or would he be open to a new future, still ready to believe in his dreams?

By the time the caravan got to Egypt, Joseph had become almost like one of the team. They gave him a coat like the other traders so the Egyptians would identify him as part of their trading team. Joseph helped the traders set up their booths along the side of the street. The peaks of the pyramids towered in the distance. Joseph wished his brothers could see him now!

The sun was only half way up the sky one morning when two traders approached. One of the traders said, "Come with us." Joseph followed. They made their way through the city, past more spectacular buildings than he had ever seen before. More than ever, he wished his brothers could see him now.

But moments later, Joseph was led through a crowd, to an auction platform where he was told, "Pull off your coat and strip to the waist, then get up on that platform." Slowly Joseph removed his traders coat and handed it to the trader, knowing what was happening – he was being sold again.

As Joseph stood there listening to the bids being announced, he began to hear a recurring bid. Suddenly it became quiet. Then he heard the auctioneer announce, "Sold." Potiphar, a member of Pharaoh's personal staff, had placed the final bid. Joseph stepped down off the platform and two of Potiphar's servants came up and led him away, still stripped to the waist. It was an intense defining moment. He had heard of slaves. Now he was a slave.

While Joseph was being led away, he began ask himself a question, '*Should I just give up and forget about my dreams? They seem like an impossible dream now.*'

The Egyptians gave Joseph the coat of a household servant and expected him to be man enough to wear it. The quality of his workmanship came to the attention of his superiors and soon he was promoted. A servant from Potiphar's big house came over to Joseph's little cottage and announced, "Potiphar wants you to come and work in his house."

There, in that elaborate new setting, the handsome young slave, who had been secured from the auction block, attracted the attention of Potiphar's wife. She flattered and teased Joseph as she pursued his attention. She wanted him to sleep with her. When she pressed what she assumed would be a weakness she could take advantage of, Joseph resisted. When she tried to force Joseph's attention, he pulled back from her. When he tried to get away, she grabbed his coat and held on to it, but Joseph slipped out of the coat and ran to his quarters.

Potiphar's wife was humiliated. She was angry and insulted to have an employee of her household staff refuse her interest. She went directly to Potiphar, holding out the coat she had wrested from Joseph as evidence, she accused Joseph of improper advances. So Potiphar took the side of his wife and not only fired Joseph, but had him put in prison.

As the big wooden door slammed behind Joseph, it was dark again, except for the light from a small hole in the door through which food was passed to prisoners. The light from the hole was even smaller than the circle of light at the top of the pit into which his brothers had thrown him. He was back.

But in the worst of times, Joseph kept doing the best of things. He looked for opportunity to befriend his fellow prisoners. One prisoner, whom he had befriended by interpreting a dream for him, had been released from prison and was soon in a position to put in a good word for Joseph. He recommended Joseph as someone who could interpret a puzzling dream Pharaoh had dreamed. So Pharaoh asked for Joseph to be brought to him.

Off with the jail coat and on with a coat in keeping with a visit with Pharaoh.

While Joseph shaved and put on a new coat, a fellow prisoner said, 'What are you doing?'

'I'm getting ready to visit Pharaoh,' Joseph said with eagerness.

'You're going to do what?' his fellow prisoner exclaimed in disbelief. 'After all they have done to you, are you going to walk right in there and act like they never did you wrong?'

'That's right,' Joseph replied. 'I am going to put the past behind me so I can put the future before me.'

When Pharaoh told his dream, Joseph knew the interpretation immediately. But did he dare give it to Pharaoh? Joseph's interpretation included advice that a reserves program be created so they could store the surplus grains in the years when they had their best harvest, then use it in the lean years, even sell some to other countries.

Pharaoh was impressed and, in turn, asked Joseph to come to the palace to set up a grain reserves program and administer it! Instead of returning to prison, Joseph was given rank and authority in Egypt, second only to Pharaoh himself.

Joseph's agricultural policy worked well! Not only were Egyptians being supplied with grain from the reserve storage bins during years of drought, but people from nearby countries were coming to Egypt to buy grain.

One day, when Joseph walked in to meet a delegation of buyers from another country, he was surprised almost beyond belief. There stood his ten older brothers! He recognized them immediately, but because of the intervening years, his Egyptian clothes, and clean shaven face, they did not recognize him.

As they bowed before Joseph, he stood in thoughtful silence. It was his chance now to pay them back, to make them taste the pit, to make them know humiliation and regret the day they had thrown him into the pit. He could make them go back home with no grain in their sacks. He had the power now! But Joseph also had another opportunity. He could choose to put the pit behind him forever, and prove to himself and his brothers that he could truly close the door on the wrongs of the past so he could open the doors of opportunity to the future.

Quietly Joseph said, "Please rise." Instead of revealing himself to his brothers, he had their sacks filled with grain, but laid out a plan to get them to return to Egypt and to bring their youngest brother, Benjamin, with them.

The brothers did return to Egypt later and Benjamin was with them. When they came in and bowed, then stood, before Joseph he could keep the secret no longer. Joseph went over to Benjamin and put his arms around him. Then he turned to his other brothers and said, "I am your brother. I am Joseph." Stunned silence followed as Joseph went to each of them and embraced them. Then he asked them to be seated.

Joseph said, "My thoughts race back across the years and distance. I don't know what your thoughts are in this moment, but I can imagine. Perhaps it's hard for you to believe this could ever happen!"

When Joseph's brothers returned home from Egypt, it was an exciting time. As soon as they got within sight of home and close enough that their father could hear them, they began to shout, 'Joseph is alive, and he is ruler over all the land of Egypt!' Jacob could hardly believe it. But after the brothers showed their father the lavish gifts Joseph had sent to him, he said, 'It must be true! Joseph, my son is alive! I will go and see him before I die.'

Before they began their trek to Egypt, Jacob went to an old trunk where he had stored some treasured keepsakes. Slowly he opened the trunk and lifted out the coat of many colors. He remembered the day his other sons had brought the torn, blood-stained coat to him, saying they had found it in a field and asked, 'Is this Joseph's coat or not?'

'Yes,' he sobbed, 'It is my son's coat.'

Joseph's father carried that dual symbol of tragedy and blessing with him as he journeyed to Egypt. When Jacob approached his son, that coat was lying across his outstretched arm. Tears streamed down his face as he said, 'Oh, my son, my son, I never thought I would ever see you again.'

As Jacob held out that special coat, he said, 'Joseph, I have something very special for you. I have the coat I gave you when you were just a boy. I saved this coat across the years as part of an unfulfilled dream. Never did I realize the dream was still being fulfilled in strange new ways and that I would have this opportunity to present the coat to you again. Truly, God has blessed beyond anything I ever dreamed, and perhaps beyond anything you ever dreamed.'

Joseph reached out slowly and took the coat He ran his fingers across the fabric, then looked up at his father and said, 'Thank you for saving my special coat all these years. I never knew what happened to it, but the memory of it has been a part of my life ever since. The confidence you showed in presenting it to me has helped me to believe in myself and to feel that I could keep following my dreams in spite of all that happened. In a sense, I have continued to wear that coat of dreams across the years.'

Judge Williams looked at his young audience and said, "My young friends, you can wear a coat of dreams all across your years. You can dare to dream a dream worthy of the opportunity that is opening before you, here and now, in the greatest age of potential the world family has ever known. It will be different for each of you, but look ahead. Dare to dream your best dream, and then give your best dreams their best chance to happen!"

CHAPTER TEN

Jonas Ridge

RU EAGERLY LOOKED FORWARD TO THE LETTERS HE GOT FROM JUNE once a week since he left Jonas Ridge and returned to the Juvenile Center. He read them with emotion and answered them with special care as a link to what was becoming more than just a friendship. They began to close their weekly letters with words of endearment and finally, 'With Love.'

As the exchange of letters extended across the year, they began to focus on their high school graduations. June sent a printed invitation to Ru, inviting him to her graduation. It would be only one day after Ru's graduation at the Juvenile Center. Ru talked to the social worker at the Juvenile Center to make sure he would be free to leave just as soon as own high graduation was over so he could be back at Jonas Ridge in time for June's graduation.

Excitement about graduation was building. For Ru it was an event that easily might never have happened. In a letter to June, he said, "I came here thinking of this being a place of punishment, when it was actually an opportunity. Still, I wonder if that opportunity would have happened on my strange journey without one special book, *NEW TOMORROWS,* where the stories were about turning old endings into new beginnings. I owe so much to many people, but none more than what I owe to you, June. Your friendship and caring love have been like a North Star, giving me hope and special dreams. I look forward to your being here for my graduation and I am so pleased that things are working out so that I can be at your graduation the next day. Along with that, I will be celebrating being back in Jonas Ridge and building plans for a new future!'"

Ru completed his senior year with good grades and marched across the stage at the Juvenile Center along with fifteen other students as a celebration. June was there, along with her parents, and watched as Ru walked across the stage to shake hands with his principal and receive his diploma.

There was a tradition at the center. Just as soon as each student received his or her diploma, there would be a moment when family and friends and others could stand and applaud in a kind of celebration. Immediately after Ru shook hands with his principal as he was handed his diploma, he looked out at the audience and saw June standing along with her parents. In that moment Ru saw another person standing with them. It was Judge Williams. They were applauding with enthusiasm. Then Ru noticed something special. With his hand held high, Judge Williams was giving Ru the thumbs up sign. Then Ru saw John and Marie Hyland, along with June, giving the thumbs up sign. What made it so special was that these were people who believed in him when it seemed like the thumbs were all down. Lifting his diploma high in one hand,

and with the other, Ru returned the thumbs up sign, as he walked off the stage to new beginnings.

The next morning, Ru walked out from the Juvenile Center to the van with excitement in his steps. He was pleased that his cottage parent, Jim Waymoth had asked to be the one to drive him back to Jonas Ridge when he left the Juvenile Center. When Jim asked if he could help carry things out to the van, Ru said, "There's much to take, but you can carry my old brown suitcase and I'll carry the old cardboard box. Explaining about the box, Ru said, "the old worn box has been me ever since I left Jonas Ridge. It was an embarrassment then; now it is a treasure, almost like an old friend."

Jim noticed Ru's devotion to the old box and asked him about it once they were inside the van. "I noticed how you treasure the old beat up box, but sense there's something special about what is in it. I could see that what you had right on top was a book, called NEW TOMORROWS, and beside that, you had some letters with a string around them, as though the two belonged together. Is there something special about that?"

"Oh, yes," Ru answered immediately. "As my cottage parent for more than a year, you already know about that special girl in Jonas Ridge, June Hyland. Those letters are from her. They are a link back to beautiful yesterdays when June and I were childhood playmates and school classmates – a treasured link to what has become a very special friendship. Like you said, those letters and the book belong together. Both helped me believe in myself and to reach beyond yesterday for a better tomorrow.

When we get to Jonas Ridge I am going to go up to June's

house and then go with her, and her parents, to her high school graduation. I just hope I get there in time"

Jim responded to Ru's anxiety by saying, "It's not far out to Jonas Ridge. Even on these crooked roads, I am sure you can get there in time. But, tell me about the book."

Ru said, "The ten stories in the book are about people who turned problems into opportunity – people who reached for new tomorrows instead of crying over lost yesterdays. I read the book while I was in the Quiet House. They helped me to believe in myself and begin to dream about a future in Jonas Ridge, once I got out of the center. So when I get back home, I have plans."

Following a momentary pause in their conversation, as they drew close to Jonas Ridge, Ru said, "Mr. Weymouth, I am grateful for how you, and all the staff at the center, helped me get my life back on track so I could move on with my best story for the promise of the future."

"Thank you, Ru, for saying that," Jim said in response. "That's a high compliment to all of us. Helping young people reach for their best dream is a part of a dream that all of us keep working on. We are a team and we want to make a difference for good in our place in the story in our time in history. Your success story is a part of that story."

The drive didn't take long and when they arrived back in Jonas Ridge, Ru asked Jim to drive past his own house, cross the bridge, go in front of Dallin's Apple Shed, and on out to his granddad's house. As soon as the van stopped, Ru was out in a flash. He paused and took a good look around before he began getting his few belongings out of the van. When Jim came around to the other side of the van, he asked, "Do you need me to help?"

"There's not much to get," Ru said, as he reached out to shake hands with Jim. Almost in tears he said, "Thank you so much for bringing me home again!"

Ru watched in a moment of reflection as the van left, going past Dallin's Apple Shed, across the bridge, down the road passed his house, and out of sight.

Immediately, Ru picked up his things and walked under the limbs of the big oak trees surrounding his granddad's house, and put his things down on the porch. At the far end of the porch he lifted a board, where a hidden key was kept. When he turned the key to the front door, it was like cautiously unlocking the door on a past that was strangely turning into a new future. Ru stepped inside and looked around for a moment, then turned and went back out and picked up the old brown suitcase and his old box with its special things, and brought them inside. As he set them down in the living room, he looked around again. It was all so much like it was when his grandmother and granddad had left it.

Ru turned and went back out. He locked the door behind him, and put the key in his pocket. He walked down the drive, passed the apple shed, then stopped for one special moment on the bridge, looking down at the water, flowing to some kind of new unknown new beginning. Then he quickly turned and began hurrying up the road to make sure he could get to June's house in time to go to her graduation. When he arrived at the Hyland home, June was walking toward the car, carrying her graduation gown across her arm and the cap in her hand. As they fell in step together, June said, "You are just in time."

Ru tenderly placed his arm around June as they walked to the car, where John and Marie Hyland were waiting to go to their youngest daughter's graduation event.

As June walked across the stage and received her diploma, it was a special moment of celebration for John and Marie Hyland. Four daughters had now walked across that stage. Following the graduation ceremony, Ru stood by with June's parents and watched as June said tearful goodbyes to her classmates and friends.

As they drove back to the Hyland home, Ru said, "Mr. Hyland, would you be willing to stop down at the school bus stop where June and I have waited for the bus many times? We can walk on from there."

As June's parents went on up the little road, Ru and June walked along slowly, hand in hand

"Ru," June said, "I am glad you didn't quit school. Even though our paths went in different directions for a while, how special it is that we got to graduate one day after the other. Do remember Mrs. Martin and how she expected us to memorize poetry. She had us to memorize Longfellow's poem, 'The Rainy Day.' It has that memorable line in it, 'Into each life some rain must fall.' But it also has that line, 'Behind the clouds is the sun still shining.' Today the sun is shining."

"I know about the rain," Ru said. "But today, we both know about the sunshine! Do you remember the day I went back to the Juvenile Center. I stopped by here and went into the house and got that book Pa had been reading, *NEW TOMORROWS,* and took it with me. That book has been a ray of sunlight for me. Especially the ten words."

"What words?' June asked eagerly.

"The Big Ten Universal Qualities. Power words that can be

chosen by anyone, anywhere, anytime. Kindness and Caring. Honesty and Respect. Collaboration and Tolerance. Fairness and Integrity. Diplomacy and Nobility. I have been trying to live by those words.

The judge who sent me to the Juvenile Center, came out to the center and taught classes on those ten words. He said, 'If you will live by those ten words they will change your life and open the doorway to success.' They have. And here we are together! It almost didn't happen. That book and your letters helped turn old endings into this day when the sun is shinning on new beginnings."

As they came to the drive that led up to Ru's house, Ru said, "I don't want to stop here. Let's stop at the bridge that crosses the creek. I'd like for us to stand there and lean against the handrail, like we have so many times before, watching the water flow from under the bridge and on its way into the unknown."

As they leaned against the handrail and listened to the ripple of the water, Ru turned and looked at June with a lingering smile. "I have a plan," he said. Motioning with a sweep of his hand, while he looked up across the hillside, he said, "My interest in continuing to clear the trees up there to make more land for cattle has changed. Instead of making space for cattle, I want to focus on restoring the apple orchard. I want to make it like it was when Granddad watched over it like it was a new garden. I want to make Dallin's Apple Shed come alive again the way we knew it. And, instead of moving back into the little house where I grew up, I want to rent it, and use the money I can get from the rent to live on while I attend our community college to study horticulture and environmental science. I want to move into my granddad's house. It's in good shape, but I want to update it some. So, I want to sell the two

Angus cows and use that money to go as far as it will to improve granddad's house."

June was looking admiringly at Ru. In return, as Ru looked into June's eager face, he said, "That's only part of the plan. The main part of the plan includes you. June, I love you and I want us to spend our lives together." Ru took both her hands in his, and said, "June Hyland, will you marry me?"

As though his question was not a surprise, June squeezed back on his hands, and without hesitation, said, "Yes, Ru Dallin. Yes, I will marry you!"

The lingering kiss, was followed by another, then another, as they stood on the old bridge and held each other in their arms.

"Now, I have another question," Ru said, "Would you be willing to wait until I can do some work on granddad's house before we get married? It may take a little while."

Looking admiringly at her future partner June said, "Yes, Ru. I'll wait. But not just, wait. We can work on the house together as, our house. And, as for your plan to go to the community college, we can go together."

"One more question, June," Ru said eagerly. "When can we get married?"

As they stood arm in arm looking up across the hillside, June said, "I don't know the exact date, but I know the time. It will be springtime. It will be apple blossom time."

SEQUELS: *New Tomorrows, Apple Blossom Time, The Future We Ask For, A Place In The Story, Eagles View Mountain, Sunrise Dreams, The New Sacred.*